Just a Few Thoughts
by
Patrick Mitchell

© Patrick Mitchell 2021

Kindle Edition © 2021

Second Kindle Edition © 2023
First Kindle Printed Edition © 2023

All Rights Reserved

Cover Illustration by Malcolm Hardy

© 2021 © 2022 © 2023

1

The sea often slammed on to the beach, but today it was perfect. There was a gentle onshore wind, giving the waves a shimmering curl in the bright sun as they approached the sand. All along the shoreline other surfers slithered to a halt, lifting their boards, and paddling back out to the breakers.

I had been out on the waves since sunrise. I was tired, but what a day! I jumped off my board and into the shallows, wading towards the beach. I had never had an ovation for my surfing. I heard a noise and looking at the dunes, I saw a figure, hands in the air clapping my exit from the sea.

The sun was low in the sky as I carried my board towards the shack, the place I called home. My path brought me in contact with my audience, who as I approached, smiled broadly.

"You're an expert surfer. I've been watching all of you, and you appear to be the champion," he laughed. "I love to see the freedom that people enjoy when they're on the ocean with their boards."

I noticed that his speech was heavily accented. The cut of him was strange to say the least, standing on a West Australian beach. He was about fifty, tall and gangly, dressed in city clothes, and on his feet dark brown brogues.

We talked for several minutes. He took a lot of interest in my board and asked to handle it. I gave it to him, and turning it over and then from end to end, he said "They've changed from my day. They are much lighter and the material is completely different."

I couldn't see that he had known anything about surfing or surfboards from my first impressions.

We talked about the waves, surfing weather, the beach. "Look come back to the shack and I'll show you some pictures of my time surfing."

"The shack?" he said.

"Yes, where I live. You can see it from here." I pointed.

I had nothing else to do that afternoon and some company would be good. We walked slowly along the beach chatting.

As we approached, I noticed a car parked down the dusty track that led to the shack.

"Your car?" I said.

"Yes, I've driven down from Perth; it took me about six hours, quite a drive."

Before we went in I noticed that the onshore wind that had been blowing had ceased, there was a total stillness, the sea was flat and the lifeguard flags were limp, silence. I looked at my companion, he was looking to sea. I had never seen such calm before, and didn't know whether I wanted him to stay. That silence had unnerved me. I gestured that he sit down. I brewed up a pot of tea. We sat not talking for several minutes, he seemed to be lost in his thoughts and I didn't want to interrupt. The sun was setting over the ocean and he walked to the veranda to watch.

"So what brings you to these parts?"

"Oh, I've always loved to watch people surfing, and be on beaches away from cities." That certainly did not convince me about this strange man.

"And I've got to get away from them,"

"Who's them?" I said,

"Oh just people."

I left it there and started to busy myself around the shack. I left him in the main room while I showered and changed. I was going out later so I hoped that he would have left. When I went back to speak to him and before I could say anything, he said "Can I stay the night here?" There was an edge of fear in his voice. I considered this request and reluctantly said that he could.

"Of course you can, you can use the room behind the kitchen, mind the spiders!"

And so my relationship with Raimund started in a surfer's shack on a lonely Australian beach.

When I returned that night, Raimund had gone to bed. I noticed several books on the table in the main room. One of the books was open where he had stopped reading. Beside the table, a small open case containing more books. I picked up one of the books. It had the name Raimund R Roello on the cover, so I presumed this to be him. It was called "Flight of the Swifts." Just as I picked it up, Raimund appeared.

"That's why I've got to get away," pointing to the book.

It was late and I wanted to go to bed but I also wanted to listen to Raimund's story.

Looking at the time, he said "I'll be leaving in the morning, but here is my address, please contact me in the next few weeks. I've got friends in Melbourne where I'll be for about a month and then I'm returning to Europe."

He handed me a tatty piece of paper with an address and a phone number on it. I was wary of pursuing this brief acquaintance, feeling uneasy about his claims of having been a surfer, and the calm before entering the shack. This eccentric man was somebody I had never encountered before.

"Jack, if you ever come to Europe you must see the swifts during the summers in the cities and towns, screaming around the rooftops. What freedom, what freedom."

He left early. I watched him drive off, the car sending up plumes of dust as he drove through the dunes. When he was out of sight I returned to the shack to ready myself for a day's surfing.

2

My life continued in its normal pattern, cray fishing and surfing. I took my catch to local restaurants and shops. They relied on me to supply them. I was well known up and down the coast as the man who lived in that shack. I had lived there for twelve years. It used to be owned by an elderly man who had fled the cities and probably the law. I had got to know him because I was always on the beach and would visit him from time to time. My visits would become more frequent as he got frailer, and then one day he just wasn't there. At first I didn't think it strange, but then days passed and I became concerned. I asked around but I seemed to have been the only person who ever visited him. Reporting his disappearance to the police, they logged it and showed little interest.

His name was Frank. I never saw Frank again. There were no title deeds to the shack, it was just there and after six months, I moved in. The shack was my shelter and grew around me. I think Frank would have been pleased. While clearing his very few possessions, I came across a note in a drawer. "Thanks Jack, I've gone to the sea." I still have that note and when I showed it to the police, it was met with a shrug.

I made it comfortable from things I had scavenged in local shops and the tide would often leave offerings. I had no need for stuff around me. I went into town to collect new gas bottles and fuel which were needed for my lighting and cooking.

About two weeks after Raimund had left I decided to contact him. My curiosity had been aroused and I phoned the number on the piece of paper.

A woman answered. "Raimund, oh yes Raimund, he left Melbourne two days ago, he said he was heading for Queensland, to stay on the coast. He loves to watch surfing you know."

"Is he coming back?"

"No, he said he was returning to Europe."

There were lots of questions I wanted to ask her, but this was not the time. "If you hear from him, tell him Jack was asking after him."

I didn't hear anything for about three months, and then a letter arrived at my postbox on the highway, postmarked Rome. I knew nobody in Rome. Before starting home I opened it and started to read.

Dear Jack,

If you are reading this, I want to tell you that I left some documents at your house. They are part of a book I am writing. I also have a copy. You remember I said that I had to get away from them. There are people who are pursuing me for what I have written. I knew I had to make two copies in case they find me. I know I have taken liberties with your hospitality by leaving a copy with you. I hope you will forgive me. It is under the dresser in the bedroom where I slept. Please read it.

I hope we will meet again soon. I plan to return to Australia in about six months. My life at the moment means I have to keep on the move, staying with close friends or seeking refuge in safe houses supplied by those friends. Thank you for trying to contact me in Melbourne. So Jack, I'm sure the surf is up!

Your friend, Raimund

I started back to the shack, wondering, thinking about what I had just read. I went straight to the room where Raimund had stayed that night. The door creaked open. I don't think I had been in the room since, maybe once. Moving the dresser across the slatted floor, I saw a pile of neatly stacked papers and a diary, untouched since the night of Raimund's visit. I picked them up. I noticed a small note attached to the pack. "Jack. Please read and one day tell me what you think."

Why had I suddenly found myself in this position? Why did he trust me with this document? Would I now become a hunted man just because I had offered somebody shelter for a night? I knew that I lived in a remote place, and that was perhaps the reason?

I sat and read . . .

I spent my schooldays avoiding the work I was set, it seemed to have no relevance to the world I was about to enter, and because of this, no one took interest in my progress. The only two subjects that interested me were art and what was called English Literature. Why did they name it English Literature? I was thousands of miles from England, but anyway I loved the subject. We covered literature from all over the world, be it Russian classics, Shakespeare, Indian classics, Chinese. Mr Gonzales, my teacher encouraged us to look beyond Europe's shores. This was not what the curriculum laid down, so he was secretive when he told us his ideas of what could also be studied. He was loved for his enthusiasm, and theatrical behaviour, and he liked me for my approach to his teaching.

My art teacher was a German lady who had emigrated with her husband to my country. She also taught music, and tutored me on the piano. Her name was Greta Franken. She dressed in an astonishing flamboyant fashion, and was often heard singing in a beautiful soprano voice as she walked the corridors of the school.

Thus Mrs Franken and Mr Gonzales were my extra eyes on the world, my motivation to become involved in the extraordinary. And then one morning they weren't in the school, nor the next morning or the next morning. Pedro, the head teacher, for that's what we called him, appeared on the morning they didn't arrive at the school. His eyes were red as if he had been crying. He was accompanied by other staff. We all assembled in the entrance hall. He just told us that they would be back in a few days. But they never did come back.

I talked to Dad and Mother about their disappearance and felt they were holding something back from me. I still had a year before leaving school, how would I continue with my literature and music without Mrs Franken and Mr Gonzales? I missed them so much. Where were they? I didn't know where they lived, I was determined to find their homes. After they had left the school, every day, and for many weeks, the school was visited by men. Men in smart suits, dark glasses and fierce faces.

I wanted to ask Pedro, he knew I wanted to know, he avoided me, until one day, I saw him in the art room. I went in and shut the door, I had to build my courage to do this. I wasn't a courageous person. "Raimund, I know what you want to say, I can't tell you. My life is in danger since Mrs Franken and Mr Gonzales have left. Your parents are friends of mine, if I tell you, they will be taken as well." He stood looking at me, I couldn't think of what to say. He walked passed me, squeezing my arm as he made his way to the door. I turned and watched him leave.

If nobody was going to tell me why my teachers had disappeared, I would find out myself, and if I was going to do this, I had to do something about my courage. I finished my last year at school. Two new teachers were hired to fill the vacancies, but I never had the enthusiasm for their teaching. They didn't have the panache that Mrs Franken and Mr Gonzales displayed. The school corridors were quiet, no soprano voice echoing through, and no theatrics in the literature classroom. The books had even been changed. We sat in rows listening to nothing but drear.

A month before the end of term, I found Mrs Franken's

home quite by chance. Travelling to school on the bus, I saw her being handled by men out of a house and being pushed into a car. I made a mental note of the location and on a Saturday after finishing my homework I went there on my bicycle. The house was behind a tall white wall and entered by an ornate gate.

My courage was no better and I stood outside the gate trying to force myself through, I eventually did. Walking to the front door, I saw an elderly man coming around the side of the house. He stopped and looked at me. I said "I'm looking for Mrs Franken, I'm a student of hers." He came closer and gazed up at me, then said "They've taken her to the facility." The way he said facility, a nothing description, a hollow word, conjuring up a disconnect with the world.

"What's your name?"

"Raimund Roello."

"Yes, she often talked about you. You were a very special student, she told me. Come in."

We went into the house, to a sitting room, that looked out on to a small garden, where there was an apricot tree, heavy with fruit. "Sit down Raimund." He walked over to a table , picked up a diary and then took a seat.

"I have been documenting everything that has been happening to my wife since she left the school. Every week and for two days, she is taken away to the facility. They are re-educating her, she must have nothing to do with music ever again. Men came and removed her piano, they searched the house and took everything to do with music, books, sheet music, everything."

"Why?" I said.

"Raimund, the fashion for ignorance, if I can call it that, for that's what it is, is sweeping through the world. Intelligence, intellect is to be dealt with and eliminated. Not only Greta, my wife, but many others have been taken away to be re-educated. The teacher, Mr Gonzales from your

school. He is dead." I gasped at this news. *"He was hanged at the facility. Greta witnessed it. He wouldn't do as they said. He was theatrical right up to the gallows. My friends often visit me and we talk about who is responsible for this terror. There are some deeply sinister people behind it, in this country and in the world."*

It was then my mind was made up after the conversation with Mr Franken. I would oppose this thinking, I wouldn't let the void of ignorance take those beloved people I knew. Little did I know that that opposition would be my life, up till now, and that I would be pursued for supporting a natural instinct in the human existence. My schooldays ended, my thoughts maturing and substance being added to them. I kept in touch with Mr Franken. I discussed with Mother and Dad, who were fearful for their lives and for good reason.

I tried to find Mr Gonzales' family. He had been written out of history, no one knew him, even Pedro, the head teacher refused to talk. Then one day while making my way home on my bicycle, I heard singing in a square near home. I stopped to listen. I knew that voice. I looked over to the church where the singing was coming from, and there was Greta Franken, a crowd rapidly surrounding her, to listen. Walking towards the crowd, that voice injected me with courage, oh yes, the courage that I needed. Her voice soared through the streets. She must have been singing for twenty minutes, the crowd continuing to swell. I saw police arrive, they tried to barge through the throng, but as Mrs Franken's voice filled the air, they started to move away, the singing had defeated them . A smile spread across my face, and that is where I started from . . .

The afternoon turned to evening, the sound of the ocean in the background. The sun set, darkness crept up. I got up and started the generator, sat back down and read on. I was astounded by the contents of this document. The idea was preposterous. Hearing a noise outside, I went to the front door with my flashlight, circled it around the front, nothing, the back, nothing. Probably an animal setting out on its night patrol, or was I getting twitched by Raimund's writing.

After about two hours I had finished. I went to the door, opened it, and breathed in the fresh night air. The moon streaked the ocean. The night was still, nothing moved. The hoot of an owl way out on the dunes was the only sound. The sky was loud with stars. I closed the door. I was hungry so I cooked up some potatoes and crays and opened a beer.

I placed the papers under a board in my bedroom and the diary on a shelf in the living room. I had no way of contacting Raimund to tell him that I had read the document. I decided to continue as normal, there was nothing to be done, and hoped nobody would come snooping.

3

I hadn't heard from Raimund for many months, and then on a beautiful spring day while snoozing after a day's fishing, I heard a car draw up behind the shack. I went out to see who was there. Two men were getting out of the car.

"We're looking for Raimund," No introductions.

"Raimund who?" I said.

"He's a friend of ours, and we know he dropped by here a few months back,"

"I don't know a Raimund," my voice rising in irritation.

"Look we know he was here." One of the men did all the talking .

"I don't know who you are talking about. I live alone here and apart from a few friends, nobody comes here."

The Talker came closer to me in a threatening manner.

His breath smelled of alcohol, he was tall, his eyes bloodshot, body odour filled the space between us. I backed away, and as I did he moved closer. I then stood my ground, he prodded me with his right hand. He disgusted me. Raising his voice and in a shower of spittle, said, "Now get this, we want to know when he was here and if he left anything with you – "

"You say you're friends of Raimund, well I don't know him, and if you are friends you show it in a strange way."

The Talker continued. "Well see if you can refresh your memory. We'll be back tomorrow for an answer."

They left. I watched the car disappear through the dunes.

I returned to the shack, went to the room where the manuscript was hidden, grabbed it, then headed for the dunes, taking a spade and metal container in which I put the papers. I dug down into the sand in a frenzy to hide the evidence that placed Raimund here. I was frightened. Frightened by the events I found myself part of. How did those men know that Raimund had been here?

I spent a nervous night. The wind rose in the small hours, I got up, took a flashlight and went down to the beach. I walked for about an hour until the first rays of the sun edged up through the dunes on to the beach, then on to the sea where it glittered on the dancing surf.

I made my way back deciding to approach the shack from a different direction, so I cut up through a little used path, knowing I had made a good decision, hearing voices and the sound of cars as I got nearer. I crept to the top of a dune and looked down on the shack. There were four cars and a group of men loitering around. I was just too far away to hear what they were saying. I watched. It was still early. I hadn't planned to go fishing today so had time to sit this one out. Several hours passed, it was hot, and there was no shade. At last they started looking at watches, got back into the cars and left. I waited and then made my way down.

I went into the shack and rummaged around for the tatty piece of paper. I found it, the telephone number and the Melbourne address. I rang the number and believed the same woman answered.

"I'm trying to contact Raimund,"

"Didn't you hear, he was killed in Rome several weeks ago!" the voice cracked with emotion.

I hadn't known Raimund well but this news downed me.

"Look I need to speak to somebody about Raimund, how well did you know him?"

"Very well, I'm his sister."

"This is Jack; I tried to contact him months ago,"

"Yes he spoke about you."

"Can I come and see you?" I was relieved to be speaking to Raimund's sister, and then she said,

"Come to Melbourne, I can't speak over the phone. You've got my address."

The conversation ended abruptly. Did she think that she was being listened to? I needed to make it across to Melbourne.

4

The next few days were busy. I organised the fishing with my good friend Joe, who lived further down the coast. He would look after the restaurants until I got back, and see that they were well supplied. I had other projects which I did when I wasn't fishing and surfing – watching and noting the passing of whales off the coast during the migration season. This led to remarkable experiences and encounters as they wound their way south. But the short meeting with Raimund was now on my mind; I booked a ticket on a flight to

Melbourne from Perth. I felt compelled to find out as much as possible about Raimund. Since offering him a refuge for a night, as that was how I saw it now, I had become more and more curious about this strange man, and had a feeling of being pulled into his life.

Joe was curious about my plans. I trusted him completely, but I felt it best to keep my plans to myself. He saw me off from the bus station where I caught the bus to Perth. From the moment I stepped on to the bus I was uneasy. Was I being followed? I was suspicious of the other passengers.

The flight to Melbourne was late taking off. I shuffled around the departure lounge. I was uncomfortable in these surroundings; I noticed two men at the departure gate; I felt conspicuous and panicky. One of the men started looking around the room. His gaze fell on me, and then away. The flight was called and I made my way through the departure gate. The two men had gone. I boarded.

I had flown before but was always uncomfortable with the process. Not only the flying, but also the checking in and the security. Here I was – perhaps a hunted man – somebody wanted to talk to me: and I was sure their intentions were not kind.

I arrived in Melbourne and made my way to an area that I knew had a good, small hotel. Always looking, I booked into the hotel and went to my room. It was now dark; I scanned the street outside my window. Nothing. I had the tatty piece of paper. I checked the address on a map of Melbourne. I would go early in the morning.

After breakfast I walked to the tram. I found the house which was out in St Kilda. It had taken me about an hour. Still watchful, nothing had raised my suspicions.

I rang the bell and a tiny woman answered, she peered up at me. "You must be Raimund's friend."

"Yes I'm Jack."

"Come in, I'm Lucia." I went in and was shown to the sitting room.

The house was an old Melbourne house from the turn of the 19th century. The sitting room was lined with books, and double doors led to a veranda and then to the garden – which was full of sculptures. Lucia followed me in and suggested that we go to the veranda.

We sat for a few moments without talking and then she said "Raimund was writing a book; in fact it was almost finished. It was full of ideas and it exposed corruption of governments throughout the world. He had a vast amount of information which he collected over several years.

"You must understand we grew up in Argentina. Our parents were taken by the regime. In our early twenties Raimund went to Europe, and I came here. We escaped really. We have a lot of information about the regimes of South America and elsewhere.

"He knew that people were out to get him. That's probably why he found himself in Western Australia, he was on the run. His ideas are completely alien to what is happening throughout the world, and he is considered a dangerous man by many. I will let you find out for yourself. I want you to find the people who killed him."

She paused.

"Why me?" I said.

"He thought a lot of you – "

"But I knew him for two days," I replied.

"He just knew instinctively when people could be trusted; he had this sense. He spoke about you a lot. He loved surfing you know. When he was a young man he used to surf off beaches in South America. He even travelled to Hawaii."

Lucia gave me lunch and we talked into the late afternoon. I told her I was expected home in a week, and would spend my time in Melbourne visiting some of the places I used to know, and looking up old friends We arranged to meet again the next day for an evening meal

I returned to Lucia as she was preparing the meal.

She said "Feel free to look round the house." A strange offer, I thought.

She went to the kitchen and I started looking round the sitting room. It was packed with books on art, on music, but perhaps the most notable section was on France and the Enlightenment. There were several shelves on the subject. I knew nothing about The Enlightenment. I scanned the titles and moved on. I wandered into the hall, more books. I went into the dining room – paintings covered the walls. South America? I returned to the sitting room and stepped out on to the veranda.

The late evening sun caught a large Eucalyptus tree standing in one corner of the garden. The evening was very still. I walked out into the garden and looked back at the house. Wooden, old and comforting.

I had supper with Lucia. I wanted to know how I was going to find Raimund's killers – and why me? I had known him for two days.

Lucia said "I just know you're the person."

5

When I left Melbourne and said goodbye to Lucia, she handed me an envelope as I was leaving. I put it in my bag. I flew back to Perth and took the bus south, back to the shack.

I threw myself on to the couch, opened my bag and took out the envelope. I opened it. It was from Raimund. Who else?

It was a long rambling letter. He talked about his

childhood in Argentina, the rabble of dictators lining up to run the country. His parents who died at the hands of these dictators. His roaming of South America.

The family name known in other South American countries. Raimund – always keeping ahead of those wishing him harm – watching for an opportunity to put his ideas to trusted people, avoiding new ideologies. There had been enough of that in the world; they only brought misery to millions.

He travelled to Europe in his twenties. Portugal, Spain, Italy and then to France; living in Paris, where he was fascinated by the Enlightenment, from which he drew inspiration. Then he wrote *The Flight of Swifts*. It was widely read especially by the Establishments of many countries. They hated it and saw it as a threat to their power and lives. This led to hatred and scorn from many in power, and he became a hunted man. The letter ended abruptly as if somebody had interrupted him. *Jack, they are near, the street lights have just gone out.*

The street lights have just gone out. What did he mean by this? I was being drawn deeper and deeper into this story. A man I had known for two days on a lonely West Australian beach. What should I do?

I visited Joe, down the beach. When I saw him he had been tending his craypots, and before I could speak he told me excitedly about the whale migration along the coast. The best he had ever seen! We arranged to meet in the shack later that day. I had known Joe for many years and, because of my trust in him, I decided to tell Joe about Raimund.

Joe arrived and I opened a couple of beers and got the barbeque going. It was a beautiful evening, the sun was setting and I could hear the cry of wading birds on the margins of the gentle surf. We talked into the night. Joe was a great listener. He allowed me to talk, there were few interruptions.

"You know, Jack, we've chosen this life. It couldn't get better out here on the beach. We have money, we walk across the beach to get to work, and the wind is on our back. You must do what Lucia asked."

We drank to that.

6

I said goodbye to my friends – Joe, Jessica (a woman who ran a restaurant on the coast. There were ups and downs, but I hoped it would come to something one day!). Joe would see that the restaurants were supplied.

I had arranged a passport, visas and travel over the month since my talk with Joe. I then flew to Paris. Paris because it was often mentioned in that letter; and I had become intrigued by the events and the thoughts that had influenced much of our life today.

I travelled light, there was nothing on me that could connect me with Raimund. The Talker was my foe; I was always on the lookout for him and his foul presence. I was constantly watching.

I knew nothing of the Enlightenment, but was willing to learn. I made my awkward way to a hotel near La Place St Michel.

In the rambling letter he had mentioned a small café near La Rue de Savoie where the owner was a friend of his. After several days of walking in the city I made my way to the café. I only had the first name of the owner, Marcel. The welcome was guarded but friendly. Marcel ushered me to a table away from the windows, gave me a coffee and some delicious croissants. We talked.

"I have known Raimund for many years. He stayed with me while he did a lot of his writing."

I told Marcel about meeting him in Australia and then going to Melbourne to see his sister who told me about his death.

"Death, what death? I saw Raimund a week ago – and he was alive then."

I was shocked. I had made my way to the other side of the world after being told that Raimund had been killed, and had been asked by his sister to find the people who had killed him. What was going on? Was this a trick? But to trick who? And what was my part in it?

After telling Marcel my story, we were silent, both of us taking in what we had told each other. "When will you see Raimund again?" I said.

"Raimund. He comes and goes, he never keeps to schedules. He might disappear for a year, and then suddenly appear. I don't have any contact, address, phone number, friends, nothing."

We sat not talking for a few moments.

"He did say he might go to Rome," Marcel eventually said.

"Rome, that's where he was meant to have died. So Lucia told me," I replied.

7

I stayed in Paris for a few days. Rome was a place I had always wanted to visit. But why did I think I could find Raimund? I had no address, I just had a feeling that I could. I booked out of the hotel, said goodbye to Marcel, took a train to Milan, and then to Rome. I found a hotel near the Trevi Fountain. I would stay a week and then return to Australia.

I walked the streets of Rome, hoping to find Raimund. I

searched through directories, but his name did not appear anywhere. On the verge of giving up and while sitting in a café I saw Raimund. I rushed after him as he disappeared into the crowds and then saw him go down an alleyway. I reached the alleyway, looked down, no sign of him. I returned to the café paid for my drink and went back to where I had last seen him.

I walked slowly down the alley looking at the doors, which one? There was a café with a good view of the alley, I ordered a coffee and waited. I didn't have long to wait. Raimund emerged from a doorway and walked towards me. Should I greet him or follow him to see where he goes? I slunk back into the shadow of an awning. He passed me. I decided to stay where I was, watching him until he was out of sight.

I finished my coffee and then walked to the doorway where he had appeared from. There were no names on the bells. I rang number one. I waited. I heard movement at one of the shutters above me. I stood back from the door and looked up. A woman was looking out of the window. She spoke to me in Italian. I shrugged my shoulders. Then she started to speak English.

"Are you Jack?"

"Yes I am."

How did she know who I was?

"Well Raimund told me to tell you to wait in the café just up there; he should be back in an hour. He's gone to the station to book some tickets."

I thanked the woman and made my way to the café. I waited and saw Raimund approaching the café. He looked serious.

"Jack come with me, we must be quick."

I followed him to the apartment building where I had spoken to the woman. We went in and took a rattling lift to the top floor. He ushered me in to an ancient apartment and shook my hand. We went into the living room.

On one of the walls was a large painting. It was of a surfer riding a giant wave. He saw me looking at it and smiled. "Sit Jack, coffee?"

Raimund busied himself in the kitchen and returned with two cups of coffee and sat down.

"My story Jack, yes my story. But first, how is your beach and your, how do you call it, your shack?"

I told Raimund about the beaches, the shack, watching the whales on their migration, the sea, my friends up and down the coast, farmers, fishermen, the Karri forests, my Aboriginal friends who when on walkabout would sometimes visit the shack and stay around for maybe a week and then move on. Where? Nobody knew, but their rhythm of the land was perfect.

I talked and talked as I watched the setting sun sink over the roofs of Rome. Raimund's face fell to shadow and I wasn't sure whether he was asleep or not. But he wasn't, a shaft of sunlight hit his face, and I knew he just wanted to listen.

After about an hour I fell silent, exhausted from talking. We didn't talk for a few minutes and then Raimund stood up and turned a table light on. He then walked over to a door.

"Jack, I want to show you this room."

I followed him in and saw the last rays of the sun swamping the room. There were shelves packed with books but also hundreds of filing boxes, there was a table and chair in the centre of the room and on the table was an open box file full of photographs and an index beside the box.

"Have a look Jack, take your time."

Raimund slipped out of the room and left me marvelling at the amount of boxes from floor to ceiling. I moved slowly around the room, reading the labels. I took a box down, went to the chair, sat down and opened the box. It was full of photographs, together with a note book. I opened the note book and leafed through it. It was an index of the photographs in the box. Most of the photographs were colour and showed street scenes, buildings, countryside, and people in crowds; people close up, animals in the forests, rivers. The box I was looking at contained photographs from Peru, exploring other boxes the photographs changed, and I put this down to the advance of technology. I must have been in the room for several hours, when Raimund came in.

"Jack you seem to be engrossed!"

I had in my hand a photograph; there was a smile on my face because it was a scene of a beach and Raimund walking up the beach with a surfboard under his arm. It must have been taken many years ago, the surfboard was of a different time and Raimund looked to be in his thirties. On showing him the photograph, he laughed. He shuffled another chair into the room and sat down. There was no need to talk about the scene; we knew what we were thinking.

"Raimund, I've travelled across the world to find out who killed you, and here you are very much alive! Surrounded by books and boxes of photographs. You must tell me who is after you. Why did your sister say you had been killed? Why are the street lights going out? And tell me about this room."

It was late now; I got up and went to the window, and looked across the rooftops. It was a beautiful night and the sounds of the city reached the room.

"First we must eat; I know an excellent little restaurant just minutes from here. I have to take some precautions before going out into the street."

Raimund left the room and appeared back several minutes later. He didn't tell me what the precautions were, but asked me to follow him. We went through his apartment and down some back stairs to a narrow street that led to a busy road. We walked among the crowds and then turned up an even narrower street and came to the restaurant.

Our conversation touched many subjects but none of the important questions. Raimund steered me off those when he thought I was about to ask. We arrived back late at the apartment.

"Jack, I'll meet you tomorrow back here, come about eleven and we will get to work."

I returned to my hotel. I wondered about work, it sounded very abstract, but I was sure that tomorrow would reveal some answers to this increasingly strange trip that I was on.

8

I met Raimund in his flat at eleven and listened and listened.

"The files, the books, but especially the files are of my time in South America. I was born in Argentina during the dark days of the dictatorships, and in my late teens started out on my travels through the continent. Travelling on foot, hitching rides on trains and local buses, recording the things I saw with an ancient battered camera which my father had given me when I was sixteen, and which I still use when I can get the film. I also wrote a long diary of my trip. It took me nearly five years, travelling in no particular direction.

"While going north I might decide I should go south again, and I did. I met hundreds of people during the journey. Many of them offered hospitality but otherwise I stayed in hotels and guest houses. I worked to fund my travels. Working on ranches in Argentina, mines in Chile, labouring on roads all over the place, and working at resorts in Brazil. And that is where I found a love of surfing. The pay wasn't good anywhere, but I made enough to get by."

He stopped talking for several minutes, went to the

kitchen and returned with two glasses of red wine.

"I wanted to travel as light as possible and I wanted to travel without a guide in the Amazon region, which was not a good idea. I eventually hired a guide, Pran, who took me into the forests where I spent a year. He took me to a tribe deep in the rainforest. A tribe that had hardly seen an outsider and this is where my life took the direction it has, and why you see me keeping to the shadows. As we approached their village, I heard the sound of humming. I thought I recognised the music but at that time I couldn't place it.

While staying with the tribe the same music was played again, in fact several times, on instruments fashioned from the forest. Flutes and drums. The music, yes that music. I spent several weeks with the tribe and one night, when in my hut and just falling asleep, the music started again, they were playing on the edge of the village among the trees – and then I knew. It was Rhapsody on a theme of Paganini by Sergei Rachmaninoff. How could that be?

"I asked Pran about it. He told me that they had been playing it for years and that every time he visited they would play that music. Pran told me that they had no connections with the outside world and that they were totally dependent on the forest. Through Pran, I asked the elders about the music. They found it hilarious that I didn't know. They just said it was a treasure from many years ago, they thought everybody knew it. There were no other explanations."

Silence, he stared out of the window deep in thought and then continued. "I must tell you I love that music. I remember my mother playing it when I was a little boy. My mother was a good pianist. I especially remember hearing it when I approached home after school. And I knew I was home. But deep in the Amazon rainforest that was very different, but was it?

"Towards the end of my travels, I contacted Pran. I wanted to go back and visit the tribe. I met him in a hotel in

Rio. As he approached me, I saw a grave look on his face and then he told me that the entire tribe had been slaughtered and that the forest had been burnt down. I visited the land where they had lived and I screamed with rage, my eyes heavy with tears.

"I would keep their memory alive. But at the back of my mind the Rhapsody by Rachmaninoff would not leave me. You know there were no graves, nothing, just burnt vegetation and bleeding tree stumps. As I was leaving the land, I was approached by several men; I was threatened, told to leave and not to return."

I could see that Raimund had been deeply affected by this. He got up and stood looking at a picture on the wall. He wiped his eyes and returned to his chair. I saw that the picture was the portrait of a young man. I didn't ask who it was, but thought it must have been Pran.

"I spent a month in Peru, one of several trips there, and was in Lima for two weeks. I was doing research on family connections and was hoping also to find out any information about the slaughter of the tribe. I was up against powerful interests.

"I would often walk to a park in the Mira Flores district, sit, drink coffee and watch the people. My attention was often drawn to the shoe shine boys: they were hardly boys since most of them were men in their forties and fifties. They were very smart, in matching uniforms, carrying the tools of their trade in a large wooden box; the box was also used as the shoe shine stand. I used to sit for an hour and noticed how customers would seek out the same shoe shiner each day.

"There was one shoe shiner who I came to know as Santos. He was a man of about fifty, tall, balding, with a face like a crumpled piece of paper and a dark moustache. He was polite and gracious and would often acknowledge me with a wave as I had become a bit of a regular to the park in the two weeks.

"Each morning choosing a bench near him, he would smile at me. His customers were many types, and while shining the shoes the conversation was intense. It was so pleasurable to watch this interaction, and I often wished that I was privy to these conversations as they looked serious and profound with humorous asides.

"When returning to my hotel one evening, and passing a small bar I saw Santos sitting with friends and as usual in deep conversation. I was tempted to go in and talk to Santos but thought better of it. I still had a week in Lima and would see him again anyway. I continued my visits to the park and then one morning Santos wasn't there. Why should he be? It was probably his day off. I approached another shoe shiner and asked him where Santos was.

"'He comes, he goes, and never tells us.'

"This didn't strike me as odd, but when I was on a bus going down into the city, I saw Santos entering a building, smartly dressed and carrying a bag, several metres behind him were two younger men. The three of them looked as though they were together and it struck me that the two men with him were bodyguards. I got off the bus near the building and walked back. It was a government building. On a plaque outside was the name *Ministry of Arts and Culture* I went in and was challenged by a doorman. I asked who the three men who had just entered the building were, but was firmly asked to leave.

"On my last evening I went to a restaurant with a friend. It was in a street off the main square of the city. On opening the door I was greeted by Santos. He must have seen the surprise on my face, but he didn't appear to recognise me.

"'Come in, this is your home, treat it as your home.'

"He showed us to a table. We had our meal; and as I was paying for the bill, Santos came to the table and whispered that he would be back in the park tomorrow.

"I returned to the park early the next morning . Santos was there sitting on a bench. I sat down beside him. He looked at me with that crumpled face and he started to speak.

"'When you first came to the park I noticed your interest in the people and the shoe shiners. I chose to do this two years ago and have met many people. I want to know what people think, about their country, about their lives, their hopes and fears. People speak to me freely. I also work as a waiter in the restaurant where you saw me, there again; they speak and tell me many things. I need to know so I can fulfil my obligations.'

"I wanted to ask him about The Ministry of Arts and Culture but didn't. I had intruded enough. It was then that my attention was drawn to two men standing on the edge of the park. They were the same men that I had seen Santos with yesterday from the bus. Santos acknowledged them, and said that he must go. 'Meet me tomorrow and I'll tell you more.'

"Before I could say anything he was gone. I never saw Santos again. At the end of my trip in South America and before leaving for Europe, I was reading a paper in Brazil and came to the obituary column. Staring out at me was a picture of Santos, described as a 'former president'. I asked a friend of mine if he was a good president. My friend said 'Too good, that's why they assassinated him.'

"Jack do you know anything about Leo Tolstoy?"

"Nothing Raimund, but I'm sure you're just about to tell me."

Raimund laughed.

"He talked about the struggle of the tender against the harsh, of meekness and love against pride and violence. That was Santos."

9

It was afternoon before we left the apartment and made our way to a restaurant for a late lunch. We left by the back stairs. We were met at the restaurant by an elderly lady, Elena, an aunt of Raimund's.

"I want you and Raimund to come to a concert with me this evening. It will be a surprise. We will meet at your hotel and make our way from there."

We met Elena and went to the venue by taxi. Of course I knew what I was going to hear, but it was the first time I had heard it. It was the Rhapsody. It was a wonderful evening and Elena was a perfect host. The next day I had to confess to Raimund that money was short and that I must return to Australia to continue my work. My flight was in a week.

"Then I have somewhere to show you before you go. My aunt Elena has a small farm in the hills south of Rome. She has suggested that we visit and stay for a few nights. What do you say?"

We made our way there by local trains, arriving in the late afternoon. Picked up by Elena's helper, Mario, in an ancient car. The farm was about ten kilometres from the station.

Elena greeted us on arrival and showed us to our rooms. Mine was at the front of the house, looking out over an olive orchard: Raimund's at the back, goats bleating under his window. We stayed three nights.

The first evening the four of us went into the village in the ancient car. Elena had reserved a table at the only restaurant. The interior was a maze of pictures, intriguing bottles crowding the shelves behind the bar, their labels the highpoint of the display. The owner greeting us like old friends, which indeed Elena was. The food nourished me after the long day. We returned to the farm.

It was time to sleep, I went to my room and while lying

on my bed I watched a spider, high up on the wall weaving a web. There was a light breeze, the curtains flapped, an owl hooted. The breeze dropped. Not a sound now. I switched off the light, the moon streaked the room. The spider had gone.

I was woken by birds, the sound of goats, rays of sunshine crossed the room.

We spent the day walking the valley, but first Elena's orchard, watching Mario tending the trees, the olives ripening. Returning in the late afternoon. Mario this time preparing the goat's milk for cheese. He showed us the beehives where Elena was working.

Back to the village and the restaurant, a pavement table laden with local produce, bottles of wine. Hoping that Elena could drive us back home, she did perfectly.

Breakfast with steaming coffee and breads .We walked again, to a river, distant views of villages, perched high on the hillsides, the crisp morning air. On returning to the house, Mario asked Raimund for help to water the vegetables. I watched as Raimund hauled the water, he seemed at ease and fulfilled with such a simple task.

The last evening we dined on the terrace of this old, solid house. The air was warm and still and the distant hills shimmered in the early evening light.

"Jack, I saw you talking to Delio, the owner of the little shop near my apartment. You know I love the small shops in my district of Rome. He and his wife Margarite have run it for many years. When I was a boy, Mother and Dad used to visit a shop in our neighbourhood of Buenos Aires, it was owned by Old Hazard. He sold everything, it was fascinating to visit. Delio sells all the food I want, I have no need to go further. Local wine, cheeses, bread, vegetables. He is a man at ease with the smell of coffee and bread! It stays open late, Margarite runs the bar at the front, laughter and good humour spill into the street.

"I often sit with Delio in the evenings drinking wine, and sometimes go with him to buy his supplies in the country or at the port. He is never in the shop on a Wednesday, I wondered where he went. His daughter is in on that day. Why should I be surprised? It's probably his day off. A Wednesday, when I am returning home, I see Delio near The Spanish Steps. He is sitting on a stool, playing the cello. A crowd is gathered, Tango dancers, lots of them. Tourists being sucked into the crowd by the music. The glee the watchers and listeners are experiencing. He has never said anything to me about his music.

"I return to The Spanish Steps the next Wednesday. He isn't there, he's in St Peter's Square, a lady at the kiosk tells me. Nearing the Square, I hear his cello. A distant Delio is surrounded by tango dancers. I look up to the rooftops, birds are ranked along the ledges, listening and watching. He finishes playing, the dancers walking away through the clapping, cheering crowds. Delio walks towards me, smiling, places his hands on my shoulders, squeezes gently, I am accepted into Delio's world. We amble through the streets: him to the shop, me to my home. The smell of baking bread from the bakery near his shop. Oti has been in Italy for years now. Eritrea, as a refugee, crossing the sea to escape a brutish leader. She's known as the black baker. Next week is my important day, come with me, I'll wait for you outside the shop.

"We go by bus to a poor area of Rome, the blocks around a rough grassed area. Delio sets up. We don't have long to wait. A hot day, a gentle breeze reaches us. Violinists, guitarists arrive, Delio greets them, then children, hundreds. They sit on the grass. The music starts, a group of children in bright costumes dance. Applauding and cheering rises in intensity at the intervals. The blocks looking down, I would like to think they are smiling. A priest standing at the edge, his hands clasped in gratitude. I return with Delio on the bus, he is silent, sadness on his face.

"'It always makes me feel like this, Raimund.'

"I go to see Delio, he is sitting outside the shop, a glass of wine in his hand. I sit with him, watching the street life.

"'Luciano, I got to know him when he became a regular at the shop, he is a poor man and comes from the district where I played for the children. The children have known nothing but poverty and he asked me to come and play and so every month that is what I do. They are Romans, Africans fleeing from persecution. While I'm playing I've seen the birds of Rome crowd the rooftops. What is it that pierces us and calls us to listen? It is a perfect time for the ragged. Listen can you hear?' Above the street sounds a violin is being played. 'It is Caria, she is fifteen and comes here to play nearly every evening.'

"Last year I went with Luciano and the musicians to villages and towns, playing in the streets and squares. The news of our arrival sped ahead of us, the places were thronged. That year there was a stillness in the land, birds multiplied, crops flourished, it enriched lives.

"Delio asked me to go with him to the coast, south of Rome. We would be away for three days. There is a natural bridge for migratory birds flying from Africa, crossing the Sahara to Italy, and then on to the north. Local buses south, bags and cello, a hotel overlooking the sea far below. 'We must be up early tomorrow, we have an hour's walk to the gap.' I started to ask a question, Delio put a finger to his lips, stay silent.

"The morning glistened as we set off through olive groves, orange groves. Narrow tracks between banks of flowers, on to a grassed hillside where we stop. He takes the cello from the case, walks to a stone and sits down. A pulse of summer heat seeps into the meadow.

"Raimund, the rock over there will give you a wonderful

view, we haven't long to wait."

"I make my way to the rock. There is a silence, the sea is flat. A sudden slap of wind, I hear the cello, and then the birds, thousands crossing from sea to land. Swallows, song birds diving and swooping. Messengers from a distant land.

"Shots one after the other. I see the guns but not the people. Birds flutter to the ground. A man appears from the trees, red faced and ranting, he yells at me, he points his gun, I flee. His friends advance on Delio, he continues to play, they surround him, his cello is wrenched away and splintered into a thousand pieces. He is beaten to the ground. I rush to help Delio. I'm prodded, pushed, shouted at. Lifting Delio to his feet ,we retreat, they swear, laugh, fire their guns over our heads. Running to the hotel, no pursuit. Exhausted, we arrive.

"We watch from Delio's room. A car passes the hotel, the hunters, no, the killers, they pass the other way. The car stops, the men get out. Standing, pointing at the hotel, smoking, talking, leering. The art of gloat. The yeller stands at the front, hands on hips, trousers tucked into his boots and around his neck, hanging on twine, dead birds. A closer look at the other four, dead birds dangling from their belts. Delio leaves the room, I hear him running down the stairs. He walks up to the five men. He stands back from them. Looking down at the ground and then he raises his head, his eyes taking in what is happening. The hotel, the rooftops of the village houses, power lines, trees, covered with song birds. I like to think they were looking down on the men. Song fills the air. The men shuffle awkwardly, hoping for encouragement, courage from each other.

"I join Delio. The hotel staff, the villagers crowd the street. Nobody speaks, just the song, the beautiful song of the birds. The men walk away, shoulders hunched, heads hanging. Need anything else be said. Delio was presented with a new cello and his streets echo to the music, the birds cross the coast, Delio playing as they fly. There is now a sculpted swallow in flight, on the cliffs flying north."

I left Rome on a flight to Singapore and then on to Perth. Raimund saw me off, he seemed to be less worried about his security the days before my flight, and he was walking openly on the streets. I felt it was the last time I would be with him. As I said goodbye he handed me a small package and then said, "Jack, be at play with everything." A man who would follow his ideas without imposing them.

I arrived in Perth after that long, long flight; I was sad, and must confess I shed a tear when leaving Raimund. He remained a mystery, I liked it that way. I made my way home; the bus dropped me off at the road to the ocean. It was about ten kilometres from the road to the shack. It was midmorning and I decided to walk. The road is paved to start with and then becomes an unsurfaced track. I meandered, taking in the wild surroundings, the sounds of the bush and then hearing the first crashings of the surf. What a contrast, Rome and this beach.

On approaching the shack, I heard music coming from the open door. It was the Rhapsody. Yes, it was unbelievable. Jessica greeted me. We embraced. I looked over to the CD player.

"How did you know Jessica?"

"Know what?"

"The music."

"I'm not sure I know what you mean." I didn't try to explain. I opened the package that Raimund had given me, inside was a CD, I would listen later.

Life became routine over the months. The CD, it was birdsong. I presumed from the Amazon, I didn't attach a lot of importance to it. Raimund was on my mind constantly for the first few months, and then the memories started to fade. I wondered about his family, a sister and an aunt was all I knew of.

I went on holidays with Jessica. We would set out in the pickup into the interior. We stopped at sunset, put a tent up, lit a fire, cooked a meal and took in the vastness of our surroundings. The enormous sky with unending stars, the sounds of the night in the bush. I would think back on those few weeks in Paris and Rome. I had to contact Lucia, but wasn't rushing to go back to the questions that had perplexed and bewildered me during those weeks.

Curiosity took hold and I phoned Lucia one evening, after returning from fishing. The phone rang for a long time and then was answered by a male voice.

"Lucia, she isn't here at the moment, she won't be back until next week."

"Tell her Jack phoned."

I left my number and kept the conversation short. He said that he was a friend and that he was looking after the house while she was away.

Lucia phoned about two weeks later.

"Can you make it to Melbourne Jack?"

I told her I couldn't, I just didn't want to leave at the moment, but said "Can you make it out west?"

"Of course I can, I just have to arrange a few things here, and I'll let you know my dates."

When she did, I booked her into the local hotel up on the main highway, thinking that if she wanted to stay with me, she should see where I lived first, and then she could make up her mind when she had seen the shack.

She arrived in December on a hot summer's day. She had taken the bus from Perth and I picked her up and took her to the hotel, an old rambling building which had been around for years. Mum and Dad used to take me and my sister there for a Sunday treat. The manager knew me well. Lucia was full of conversation, but didn't mention the main reason for her visit. Leaving her at the hotel I said I would be back in the evening to take her to the beach for a meal. I was nervous about what she would tell me because it was now months since my return from Europe.

I picked her up that evening and brought her back to the shack. She loved it from the moment she saw it. Jessica was there and they immediately fell into conversation, I was glad. After the meal, we went into the living room. It was a blustery night, the wind was coming off the ocean and the shack creaked and groaned. It always gave me a comforting feeling being inside when the elements threw their forces on to the land.

We settled down to listen to Lucia. Jessica knew about Raimund , but so far I hadn't told her much.

"He left Rome several months ago now and travelled back to South America. There was a time when he felt more confident about his safety, but now he has received some threats when his pursuers found out where he was living. Before he returned to South America he went with a friend Alain to Berlin. Alain was presenting a talk on the establishment within Europe and the corrupt practices that are part of the establishment. They had taken the night train from Paris to Berlin. He loved travelling by train. They had a compartment between them and after a meal in the dining car, they went back.

"He found it wonderful to be able to travel over borders without checks. But this changed when he noticed a couple being questioned in the corridor; they appeared to be having their identities checked. After some time the questioners and the questioned left. It was now dark and Raimund spoke of Europe. It was near the anniversary of the Berlin wall falling and he believed this had been a great chance for Europe to unite and shake off the hundreds of years of slaughter. He wanted to see where history had collided with the city. They settled for the night. The train would arrive early in Berlin." Lucia fell silent as she collected her thoughts, listening to the shack creaking in the wind.

"He was woken in the early hours by knocking on the door. Alain opened the door and two men came into the compartment. They spoke to him in French. Alain started to get dressed and while doing so he slipped Raimund an envelope. He followed the men into the corridor. The train stopped. Raimund looked out into the night. There was a short platform and he saw Alain between the two men being led away. Alain looked back and Raimund saw fear etched on his face. He disappeared into the station building and the train started to move off."

"He opened the envelope.

"'If anything happens to me please contact my wife.' There was an address and telephone number and nothing else.

"He continued to Berlin, went to the hotel that they had arranged and immediately phoned his wife. There was no reply. He tried numerous times, but never any reply, so he flew to Paris that same day. He went straight to the apartment which overlooked The Seine in the Pont Marie district.

"The lady who answered the intercom was at first reluctant to see Raimund, but after he had told her who he was she came down to meet him. She finally asked him up to her apartment. She was expecting the worst and told him that she thought something like this would happen, as he was going to present his findings at a conference in Berlin. Her husband Alain had collected a lot of information on corrupt politicians and had with him a list of those people.

"'That is why he was taken.' His wife said. She had an exact copy of the document in case anything happened. While he was there, the intercom of the flat sounded. She went out into the hall to answer it. He couldn't hear what was being said, but she hurried back into the room, went to a cupboard, opened a safe, took out a folder and gave it to

Raimund. She said to him 'Take it and leave immediately. You know what to do with it. Take the stairs.'

"As he left the apartment, the folder clutched in his hand, he heard a lift door open. He rushed down the stairs and out into the street. That is why he has fled Europe. The folder, he sent it to a contact in Berlin, that contact is now dead, shot by unknown assailants and the information in that folder has disappeared."

She paused. She handed a notebook to me which she had written. It was about Raimund and part of his time in Europe. She said, "Read it sometime Jack.

"He moved everything to Colombia, his books, his pictures, research papers; he even took one of the apartment doors. I've no idea why. He said it was like a notebook to him! He lives on the coast. I've seen pictures of the house. It is old and very ornate, it is Raimund."

Lucia produced some photographs from a bag and handed them to me. Pictures of the house with Raimund standing in the foreground, and a picture of him with a woman.

"Who's the woman Lucia?" I said.

"That's his wife." Lucia replied.

"But she has never been mentioned before."

"She is from one of the tribes, from the highlands in Colombia. She's an intriguing woman."

"And what about children?" I said.

"There is a daughter who tends a garden in the highlands. She makes chocolate and sells it in the towns."

There was silence while I took in what Lucia had told me and I then said, "Lucia you must tell me why people are threatening him. I know he has written books, there are so many things I don't understand, so perhaps – " Lucia interrupted.

"Jack, I don't know myself! I was hoping you could tell me after seeing him in Rome." Apart from the room filled with books papers and photographs, I was no further forward in understanding him. And of course the Rhapsody, where did that come into the story?

"Jack, he remains a mystery to me and, when I met you, I knew that you would find the answers."

"But why me?"

"I just know."

I got up. Jessica said she was going to bed. I went to the door and looked out into the night, the wind had calmed, the ocean was still, I turned back to the room. Lucia sat silently with her chin resting on her hands. "He's coming to Australia in January," she said. "He wants to see you."

I drove Lucia back to the hotel and returned. I lay awake thinking about Raimund. Would this be a good time to forget Raimund, and avoid him when he arrived? No, he was my friend, why would I want to do that? Lucia came to stay in the shack for a few days. I went out in the boat while she wandered the beach, she made herself busy in the evenings cooking meals, and then she abruptly left.

I got in from fishing and found a note on the table. Jessica had been out at her restaurant.

I read the note. *'Jack, I'm going back to Melbourne, Raimund will be in touch, thank you for everything. I know you will find out. Lucia.'*

I read the notebook that Lucia had given me.

He stayed in Paris, but his determination to find that document drove him on. He felt a deep shame that the contact had been murdered and he believed that tentacles were reaching out from many countries to ensnare and stifle the thoughts and aspirations of those speaking out against injustice.

He returned to Berlin. Alain had vanished. That was hard to believe; there must be somebody who knew where he was. He knew where the conference was meant to have been, and went to the building, expecting a modern purpose built venue. He found a small dilapidated apartment building. It matched the day, grey, cold, forbidding. The front door was open, he went in.

A bent-over spidery caretaker asked him his business. The smell of onions cascaded out of the door from where the caretaker had emerged. Raimund looked in, a picture of a man staring out was hanging on an opposite wall, he was dressed in Nazi uniform.

"I'm looking for Alain." It was a shot in the dark.

"The wise have gone." The caretaker said.

He saw Raimund staring at the picture and started to say something but broke off. "Alain, Gertrude, Gunther, Patrice, they never come here now."

"Do you know where Alain is?"

"No, he was warned to stay away," he shrugged his shoulders. "They knew too much. Gunther died soon after they were warned. Who are you anyway?"

"I'm a friend of Alain. I knew him when I was in Paris." Raimund hoped that this would allay any suspicions he might have."

"Follow me."

Raimund followed the caretaker through a labyrinth of passages, down a flight of stairs, across a courtyard to a basement apartment, where he produced a bunch of keys, unlocked the door, and beckoned Raimund in. They went in, down a passage and into a large sitting room. A table dominated the space, armchairs surrounded the table.

"This is where the resistance was being planned." The caretaker swept his arms around the room.

"What resistance?" Raimund asked impatiently.

"How much time have you got?"

"Several days. I am staying in Berlin and then leaving Europe".

They stood in silence and then the caretaker said, "Alain

spoke of you and I am glad you have come. You are the conduit and will carry the resistance forward."

Raimund, taken aback by this burden, sat down in one of the armchairs and looked up at a picture on the wall. It was a picture of his mother and father pointing their fingers at *Stifling Conformity.*

Raimund looked towards the caretaker who was smiling and who said, "you see, you must carry it forward. That's what Alain and the others were attempting to break."

"How do you do that?" Raimund questioned.

The caretaker tapped his temple. *Stifling Conformity* – the phrase reminded him of a time in America where he found himself in a small town in Idaho on his way to San Francisco. He was a stranger in that town, and soon found out that strangers were not welcome. *Run out of town*, isn't that what they say? A baton had been passed to him. It sounded very abstract.

"All I know is Alain is somewhere in Spain. Can you believe? In this age, a person fleeing for his life in Europe, because he says things which people do not like, or writes books which do not conform," said the caretaker, shrugging. He was very good at shrugging. Raimund took his time in answering,

"Who are Gunther and Patrice?"

"I don't know but they're dead!"

Raimund gasped at the answer. "But why?"

"They were arseholes, so a man told me who visited this building,"

"But, but why?"

"They were arseholes. That's all I know."

"And did you believe this man?" Raimund said.

"No, of course not."

"Do you know anybody who is connected in any way to these arseholes?"

"Yes, Freddie Funten, he runs a bar in Berlin near to

Alexanderplatz. I wouldn't go there, it is often raided by the police."

"Before I go, who is the man in the photograph in your apartment wearing the Nazi uniform?"

"That's no man, that's my mother, she was a cross dresser. She used to act in the small theatres before the war, sneering and laughing at the regime. She was shot by Hitler's creeps, because she wouldn't fucking well conform."

Raimund placed a hand on the caretaker's shoulder as he shrugged. "My name is Pieter, keep in touch and tell me how you get on."

As Raimund left he looked back at Pieter, his eyes were brimming with tears, his parting words, "Dad was a good guy as well, do something for them."

Raimund stayed on in Berlin and went to Freddie Funten's bar. It was in a dark, drab side street. He could hear it before he could see it, music was pounding down the street. He went in.

Freddie was behind the bar and when the music stopped, Raimund went up to him. "Pieter told me about you, I'm looking for Alain."

He eyed Raimund, and then took a book from behind the bar, which was a photograph album. "What's your name?"

"Raimund Roello."

He flicked through the album and then held up a photograph of Raimund. "You're welcome Raimund."

"Where did you get that photograph?"

Freddie smiled, "From Alain of course. Look come back tomorrow. We'll talk then, but I warn you, we are being watched all the time. It's the Americans now, sometimes it's the British, then the French, even the Russians are showing an interest. Alain is a good man. His family have fled to Spain. See you tomorrow."

Raimund left the bar, keeping to the shadows and

returned to his hotel.

And there hangs the tale. He returned to the bar the next evening. The music was sombre from within, the door was locked, he knocked and after a few minutes Freddie opened the door. He was taken to a table on a small gallery that looked down to the bar and other tables. His eyes adjusted to the dark. Freddie was behind the bar. He sat for a time and then started to take in his surroundings and what he saw astonished and frightened him. Writers and philosophers appeared before him, it was a gallery of the last century. Those who had influenced our thinking and spread ideas. He must be losing his senses. He got up and moved among the tables and then near the bar, the vision was the same. He went to Freddie.

"Why not Raimund? Their ideas live on and you must carry those ideas on. I think we'll get a police raid tonight!"

Raimund didn't wait for the police raid, he went back to the hotel. He had much to think about.

He went to see Freddie the next day. He reached the street , the bar had been demolished. A space between the buildings greeted him. There was no one in the street, no one to ask, no one interested. A woman appeared, she was weeping. He approached her and saw her placing a piece of paper in the void on the rubble and then quickly walk away. He walked to the place where she had placed the paper and read, *'You will win because you have an abundance of force, but you will not convince. To convince you need to persuade, and to persuade you need something you lack, reason and right in the struggle.'*

What about Freddie? He asked. Nobody knew him, or didn't want to say they knew him.

He returned to the void a number of times over the days in the hope of seeing Freddie. When he visited, nobody was ever in the street. He asked in the cafes and bars in neighbouring streets. Many of the owners had known

Freddie. Nobody knew where he lived, except, yes, except a woman who was in one of the bars and overheard the conversation between Raimund and the owner; and, just as he was leaving, she tugged him by the sleeve to get his attention.

"I know Freddie." She said. "He lives over there." Pointing to a house which appeared to carry its dilapidation proudly between the smart blocks of apartments.

"Do you know him well?" asked Raimund.

"Everybody knows him well. He has lived here all his life, first under the communist regime, and now whatever regime this is. Nobody will ever admit to knowing him. The authorities hated his bar, always threatening to close it down. Now they've demolished it, all because of the philosopher evenings. He wouldn't open the bar on some evenings, but the talk was that he had gatherings of long dead philosophers. How can that be? Anyway that was the talk and I can believe it. Freddie was like that."

Raimund thanked the woman and went over to the house. He knocked and heard movement behind the door. Freddie opened the door, his face was drawn and pale, there was discolouring around his left eye. "Come in Raimund."

He went in and was shown to a small sitting room. They sat down. Silence. Freddie was gathering his thoughts.

"I was arrested Raimund. They took me to an airbase somewhere outside Berlin where I was questioned for hours. American, English, I don't know, they were very violent towards me. They wanted to know about the philosopher's evening. I didn't tell them anything. I was brought back here eventually. Nobody identified themselves to me, no reasons were given for my arrest."

Freddie was an illusionist. He travelled with circuses in Europe and beyond. It was said that he entertained presidents and prime ministers of all political persuasions, but his criticism of some of the regimes he performed for, got him banned from those countries. His audiences dwindled. Fidel Castro loved him and would fly him to Cuba with his troupe. Freddie loved Fidel!

There were illusions that people were astounded by. He could magic people out of thin air, figures from the past. It was strange and unsettling, but there were always shouts for more. He settled in Berlin where he opened his bar. There was an enormous interest in books on philosophy, because of him, and his philosophy evenings attracted people from all over the continent.

The authorities finally heard about the goings on at the bar. At first it was left alone, but then the police started to visit. They appeared on a philosophy night. They mingled with the figures on the floor; and were so terrified they fled.

Alain had been a frequent visitor to the bar and they became close friends. Alain encouraged those who came to the philosophy evenings to spread the word. The bar became known as *'The Berlin Bridge.'*

" Alain, you were looking for Alain weren't you? He's in Spain, his wife has joined him there."

Raimund left Freddie, the philosopher's evenings and Berlin. He took local trains through Germany, France, Spain, arriving in Madrid and found Alain.

Alain was frightened for his wife, his family, his life. "I just want to keep low for the moment. The people after me and others won't stop at anything. They have no compassion or decency, they want to wreck for their own personal gain. They are the enormously wealthy, politicians, industrialists. I'm sure I'm being watched for what I've said and written. Freddie's philosophy evenings, they really sent them into a spin. Stay, but go soon."

He stayed on for a few days. The philosophy evenings, and having been at one of them, he couldn't shake it loose from his thoughts. Just what did go on during those times?

He would never find out. But he believed that the philosophers were reigniting their thoughts and ideas and attempting to remind us. How had Freddie conjured this? Did it matter? He had, and it was upsetting many. Raimund now had the burden of passing on some of that thinking; a flame had been passed to him. It was time to return to Colombia. He never found the document containing the information about the corrupt figures among us.

10

How many times have I settled into my routine, only to find Raimund coming back into my life? And this time he did it with a theatrical flourish. I saw him approaching on the track surrounded by my Aboriginal friends. They had painted their faces with their tribal markings and were humming in a low deep throaty sound. He was in the middle of the group with a wide grin on his face.

When I was eventually alone with him my manner was brisk. "Raimund, I have to continue with my life here. I can't just go off on one of your journeys wherever it might take us."

He then said, "There is a trip I must take, you are welcome to come with me, it means staying on these shores, travelling mostly on foot, will you come with me?"

That was it.

"Where? Why? What for? and when?" I said, the irritation must have been noticeable, but he remained calm.

He put his hand on my shoulder and said, "Let's sit and I'll tell you about it.

He sat opposite me. "We will travel to the desert, and I have asked some of your Aboriginal friends to come with us."

So I had already been included in this trip.

"I have been unable to do a journey like this because of borders, wars in other countries and hostility from authorities, so I think that I can make this journey here without any problems from anybody, and would like you to come with me to where some of the most ancient people live."

We spent days talking about the journey. I had a lot to organise if I was going to be away for a couple of weeks. In the evenings I again listened to some of the journeys that he had made, and I remember one particular journey that he had made to Cambodia.

"Jack, I went there to study the ancient Buddhist texts and in those days the countryside was a tapestry of peace and small prosperity. Needs were supplied from what was grown and from the small workshops. The tinkle of bells could be heard throughout the countryside as the monks walked between the paddy fields, going from temple to temple. They asked for alms when they entered the villages where women weaved and cleaned and cooked while the men tended the fields. Chickens and pigs squawked and snuffled their way round the low thatched houses.

"Passing a temple the smell of incense gathered in the air and the low chant of the monks added to the silence. The light was brilliant and the vegetation bowed to the heat. The chatter of birds and the howl of the gibbons was an ever present companion. In mid-afternoon thunder clouds would pass overhead bringing the rain which fed the fields of sparkling rice, and as suddenly as it came it would be over and the countryside would settle after the torrent.

"It had been like this for years; modernity had hardly touched the interior. The rhythm continued in a way that could last for many more years. But there were changes, not in the villages; news was filtering through from the cities of upheavals. There was talk of people leaving the cities because of war. The villages only had a crude form of communication so it was difficult to find out what was occurring. The sense of security and isolation changed the day a long line of military trucks moved along the once quiet winding roads. They seemed to be going towards the jungle-clad mountains further north in the country.

"There was excited chatter in the villages, but the appearance of these trucks soon faded in the memory and life. The villages, the monks, the paddy fields returned to a quiet purposeful repose looked over by the spirits of the ancestors. Death was an important part of life and you would see the dead being carried to the funeral pyres led by a monk beating a gong as the procession made its way through the fields. The villagers looked to the spirits for guidance and protection, and this often required a shaman to visit households and administer to the sick or walk the fields calling up the spirits to help when harvests were poor.

"Strangers and those on pilgrimage to shrines would often pass through the country and would find hospitality when looking for somewhere to stay for the night, either in a house or one of the temples.

"The appearance of the trucks, now many months in the past, remained in some memories and they felt it was a bad omen, and so advice from the shaman was sought in many of the villages. Meetings were held, which were filled with debate, argument and discussion, and lasted over weeks. The shaman listened patiently and, after everything had been said, withdrew from the villages. This was a time for him to think deeply about what he would do. There were now more signs and events outside their daily lives. Large formations of aircraft flew high over the country and the trucks came again. The trucks would stop sometimes and the soldiers were aggressive and hostile, demanding provisions.

"It was at this time that the shaman was seen walking

through the fields, stopping at buildings, at the corners of fields, looking skywards, pacing the ground as if measuring. He spent days covering the country and then he disappeared. Word went round that the shaman had gone. A deep feeling of fear spread through the villages. And then they came, first the trucks and then the marching soldiers, and aircraft in the sky. They approached the villages. The villagers watched, and then their attention was drawn to the trees. A large black mass was gathering: gibbons, thousands of them, and then a mighty howl filled the air. The soldiers stopped, gaped and fled, trucks scattering the foot soldiers who were too slow to flee.

"A silence filled the countryside, the villagers stood motionless staring in the direction of where the rout had happened, and in the distance they saw the shaman walking away towards the jungle, he turned, raised an arm in farewell, and disappeared."

11

Our journey started on a warm winter's day. We met Jim and Sam, two of my Aboriginal friends. They were waiting for us further up the coast and from there we drove. We drove for four days to the north. We stopped at night, set our tents, cooked, talked, slept until the sun rose, and then continued.

Raimund knew exactly where he wanted to stop. We stopped at Cape Leveque with the Great Sandy Desert at our backs. We set up camp looking out on to the Indian Ocean. It was a wild place, and Raimund appeared to blend into his surroundings as if he had known this wilderness all his life. "It is a place where the past echoes through the land. The ghosts of another time are still the custodians, and you can hear them on the breeze as you sit and watch, but much more than that, they allow you to enter their door and look. Come, and we'll see."

We walked the beaches and the hinterland for days after our arrival and then, while the four of us were sitting on a bluff overlooking escarpments which stretched to the ocean, I had a strange feeling that I was able to see back in time to when the land was first inhabited. I looked across to Raimund, Jim and Sam, and saw that they were also looking into the deep distance. The feeling continued and I was then aware of finding myself on a small beach.

The day was hot, the light sparkled, the bush crackled. Strange smells surrounded me. I was at the back of the beach where the bush stopped and the sand started . . .

I saw two men in a dugout coming to the shore with a catch of fish. A woman appeared from a rough shelter and walked down the beach to meet the men. There was talking and laughter as they pulled the craft on to the sand, and secreted it amongst the foliage. I then saw the woman go to the shelter and appear with a baby girl in her arms.

During the afternoon, there was a lot of activity on the beach. The two men were packing their belongings, making bundles of their few possessions. Fish drying on poles were placed in a reed basket. They were on the move. Swallows swooped. They skimmed and acrobated their way, finally disappearing over the bush. The two men took a lot of interest in the birds. Maybe it was a sign now to leave their beach and move to a different place. A migration.

Night fell; a fire was lit among the trees, the temperature dropped. There was the sound of voices on the breeze. The night was black and the sky screamed with stars. The ocean lapped gently.

The vast orb of the sun marched into the sky, waking the dwellers, insects shattered the stillness of the morning, then sudden silence as if there was an intruder, the hesitant start of the chorus again.

The two men and the woman were busy near the shelter; the baby lay on some leaves. After several hours, with bundles on their backs, the baby strapped to the front of her mother, the group walked along the beach and into the bush. They walked with a simplicity of movement, they glided, they were part of the land, the land allowed them to pass. The small group fitted into the landscape, there was nothing out of place, they belonged among the thorn bushes, the rocks and the sand. The high ridges they passed under invited free passage.

They continued all morning over the landscape and finally stopped and settled into a huddle with the baby in the centre. The men took items from their bundles and started to eat. They slept.

The sun was low in the sky when they continued on their way. After a few hours they went into a cave at the side of the path. Darkness fell swiftly. There was flickering deep inside the cave, a fire produced dancing shadows on the cave walls. Warmth and safety from the night outside.

The dawn spread across the land, shadows rose, the cliffs, gnarled trees, rocks like a stooped congregation gave thanks to the dawn. The travellers appeared from the cave. The cave revealed its secrets. A short passage opened out into a vast chamber. A shaft of light shone in from the entrance. There was evidence of fires where people crouched for cooking and warmth. There were vast paintings on the walls. Hunting scenes, celebratory scenes and warlike encounters.

The group moved through dense bush on a rough track. A track used by generations of humans and animals. It crossed other tracks. They entered lush growth and before them a glistening pool of water, fed by a river which ran down from an escarpment. The track climbed the escarpment but the group stopped and went to the water. They drank and washed in the river, taking their time, relishing the coolness of the water on their bodies which shone in the sunlight. The baby was swung through the water by its mother. There was the sound of laughter from the adults and squeals of delight from the baby.

It was time to leave. They gathered the few possessions and started to climb the escarpment. Their limbs were used to the climb, they looked relaxed. The heat of the day smacked into the dense foliage and things cracked and groaned in that heat, small animals scuttled, rocks radiated. The travellers loped through the wild land towards a never ending horizon. The day started to cool and it was time to find a place to spend the night. They stopped in a clearing. A soft breeze jangled through the surrounding trees, the tall grass bent to the breeze as they gathered at the edge of the clearing. The place had been used many times before. There was evidence of previous travellers.

The night fell. There was the soft hum of conversation around a small fire. They were far from the sea now which had supplied the fish and which they had relied on for food. The two men slid away from the fire into the darkness, their shadows melting in the fire. Twigs snapped as they walked into the bush. The woman was left with the baby silhouetted by the dancing flames.

Suddenly the men hurried back to the clearing. There was anxious conversation. The men threw sand on to the flames, the woman gathered up the baby and they disappeared into the night. There was the sound of approaching feet. A group of men came into the clearing. They talked and inspected the now dead fire. One of the men knelt on the ground and pointed in the direction that the group had taken. They left. They were swallowed by the darkness. There was silence.

It was daylight, the two men, the woman and the baby

were moving quickly through the landscape. The pursuers could not be far behind, but there was no sign of them. They had escaped. Over the days the little band continued into the interior. They were on their guard, searching behind for the pursuers. As they walked, the bush closed behind them, only the sounds of wind, birds and the hot crackling undergrowth accompanied them on the journey.

Days after fleeing they arrived at a settlement. They were warmly greeted by the people. There was laughter and gleeful cries of welcome. The settlement had many huts and was enclosed by large shady trees. Men, women, children sat, stood and wandered from hut to hut. They gave news to each other, gossiped. They were offered food and drink.

There were many paths converging on the settlement. It was a crossroads for the people from the surrounding lands. They came here on their migrations. It was where news, views, ideas were exchanged. People stayed for a few days, they replenished and moved on. Different people from all over. There was a tall graceful man who walked the clearing. He was known by everybody and as groups moved on; he walked with them to the start of paths and waved them off. There was an energy amongst the gathered, friendships were rekindled, gifts exchanged, scores settled. The canopy of night arrived and the travellers lit fires. Small bands huddled and cooked food. A wind blew up, a sudden chill, the seasons were changing. People moved off to the huts for the night. The embers died. Silence and darkness blanketed the settlement.

The morning was cold. The threesome and the baby made preparations to depart. The morning birds flew over, their wings chopped the air. Others emerged from the huts, some walked off into the bush to shit and then to wash in a small pool fed by a stream.

They left the crossing of the paths, said good bye to friends. The tall man accompanied them down the path; and, at a large boulder, he linked arms with each in turn and left them. They moved off into the land again. They had few possessions, just what was absolutely necessary, a roll to sleep on, and reed containers for food.

The nights were cold now. They cleared ground, set out their rolls, from which they took some material in which they wrapped themselves for warmth. They gathered vegetation for a fire.

For days they continued walking until they reached a flat plain which stretched to the banks of a river. There were huts near the river and a crowd of people stood listening to a man. The man kept pointing in one direction and showed the crowd things he had taken from a bag. He held them up, dried fish, shells, fruits. Many of the people were diseased and some were injured, showing gruesome welts on their arms and legs. They greeted the three travellers and for the first time names were mentioned, Plin, Tub and Grith the travellers. Plin and Tub the two men also showed the crowd dried fish and shells. Plin, Tub and Grith had been sent out to discover new land and they were now telling the villagers about their finds. These people were being attacked by others and their land was being taken.

There was urgency among the people. After Plin and Tub had finished speaking, and showing what they had found, there was an immediate dismantling of huts, of packing meagre belongings. It was already late in the day. Women rushed to catch the children, men loaded wooden frames and they were gone.

The evening wind blew over the site, it rattled the undergrowth, it disturbed the gentle flow of the river. Men entered the abandoned place and moved among the old fire sites. They were too late; the people had moved on, away from danger.

An ochre sunset sat over the land. The tribe had stopped for the night. They scraped the ground to make sleeping areas and fire places. It was now dark. Cooking smells filled the air and as the flames died and food had been eaten, they went to the sleeping places. There was silence, not a murmur of wind, only night sounds. They slept.

Shadows in the dark, picked out by the rising moon, darted from rock to rock, tree to tree, bush to bush. Danger surrounded the camp. The tribe was unaware. They had placed no guards, trusting in the night to protect them. The massacre began. Screams woke others. There was a stampede to grab children, belongings, and those that lived disappeared into the night. The howling of victims pierced the air, then silence.

Hours later the dawn revealed the horror of the night. Wailing filled the air. The living hid in a stand of trees. Plin and Tub were there but there was no sign of Grith and the baby.

They sat sullen and dejected. They mourned; a low sound came from them, sobbing. No more than thirty were left; they knew they must hurry on before another visit from the dark shadows.

The tribe made their escape to safety. They carried the injured. Grith was among them and she was hugging a lifeless form to her breast. Her face was worn with grief. Tub and Plin urged the tribe on and as evening approached they found a hidden den, high up, away from their attackers looking down on the hostile places. Plin and Tub gently took the dead baby from Grith. They took the little body some distance and placed it under rocks. They returned to the tribe. Rations were shared out and they prepared for the night. The only sound was that of an owl somewhere in the bush. It kept up its lonely sentry duty and then left to continue its night wanderings.

The next morning the tribe walked purposefully over the land until they reached a meeting of tracks. There was hurried talk between Plin and other men before they started off on a densely forested track, which rose towards distant hills. They were safe in the hills, safe from the shadows. They entered gorges with fast flowing rivers and tumbling water. There was abundance in this part of the land. The trees were laden with fruit, the bushes bursting with berries. It was time to stop and rest. To build a camp, to wonder their future after the massacre and to move when the will was ready.

The tribe spent many weeks among the gorges and the forest. Their spirits were lifting. Food had been gathered, fruit dried, small animals trapped. It was time to move.

The morning scraped over the rocky pinnacles, the sun squeezed through the rocks. The tribe was on the move, out on to the flatlands and among the desert colours. They moved quickly.

12

The sea. They had made it. Plin and Tub rushed to the edge and splashed themselves, laughing and shouting. Grith followed slowly. The others back in the trees, watching. They were hesitant, the sea was another world. Their world was the deserts and the forests. Plin beckoned. They slowly approached the sand. The children broke from their parents. They ran to the water and soaked themselves in the shallows. The parents were cautious approaching the water, the old people preferred to sit and watch.

The children dug in the sand screaming with delight. Sand was thrown into the air as they burrowed and slithered. The parents dipped their toes in the water, broad smiles covered their faces. The old people approached the water.

The tribe started to walk the new country. Some walked

on the beach, others went into the forest. There were many things to look at, the trees, rocks, different birds, the roar of the sea smashing against the reef far out.

They must gather and plan. Tub and Plin approached the elders and huddled among the trees and bushes. Their conversation was low. They broke up and there was a lot of activity as each person started their allotted task. Ground was cleared above the sand and the building of shelters started. Days passed and a village was constructed. Food was gathered, hunting, picking, digging.

Then one morning an old man appeared on the beach. It was the middle of the morning when he came, he was small and wiry, tight grey hair, he was naked except for a cloth covering his waist. He went to a group of children playing; one of the children looked up and ran to the village. Plin appeared and greeted the man He raised his hand but they kept a distance.

The man signalled for Plin to follow him. Plin was not sure, but then he did. They walked away among rocks, Plin kept several paces behind. They walked for many minutes and arrived at a rough shelter. The man gestured towards the forest which now rose steeply from the beach. He smiled and gestured again and immediately started climbing through the undergrowth on a faint path. Plin followed. They were soon in a clearing surrounded by giant trees. It was loud with insects in the hot air. The man started pulling at the forest debris and slowly the prow of a canoe appeared. He made signs for Plin to help and soon they had uncovered the canoe. It was vast. Covered with intricate carvings.

Plin started to follow the man again to a part of the forest which was covered by mounds. It was the burial place of his people. Why had he survived and what had happened to the people? Plin had to communicate somehow with the man. He continued to follow; they reached the shelter on the beach.

"They came from the sea, they killed everybody. I was in the forest when they landed. We used to travel the coast, fishing, growing our food. We would move on after several seasons to a new place. A new place that was an old place. We always returned to our sites when they had become young again. That's the way it was. They told us we must settle, stay in one place. We wouldn't, so they killed us. Baco, our elder, escaped and told me to go before he was hunted down and killed. They then left in their boats and have never returned. The canoe in the forest was for celebrations, but we never used it. We were killed before we could take it to the sea." The old man stopped speaking.

Plin returned to his people and spoke with them about what he had been told. "We must return to our land, we know nothing of the sea." An elder said.

"Yes. The same will happen to us," another replied.

Plin was irritated by this talk. "You've got short memories; most of us were massacred, driven from our land. Tub, Grith and I went out to find a safer place to live, and we found this place. We must learn about the sea and the forests. The old man can help us."

There was conversation between the people. Grith walked from where she had been sitting with the other women to the centre.

She started to speak. "My baby was killed. I've come here to start again, away from the dangers. We have a lot to learn and if we stay together we will soon understand the sea, we can learn from the old man. If we return there will be more killing until none of us are left. We can travel the coast, build canoes, travel the rivers. We are people that can survive because we move. Because we move. We must learn."

Grith stepped into the background. There was astonishment on the faces of the adults – a woman speaking to the tribe. Moments passed and suddenly the women raised their arms and let out yells in agreement. Their faces broadened with glee, they crowded Grith, clapping their hands. The men skulked. Plin's face was beaming.

13

The old man was welcomed into the tribe. He spoke to the tribe using his own dialect, hands, waving of arms. The word *Drent* was often used, which the tribe took to be his name.

The evening, and insects danced in the still air. Everybody was round a roaring fire. Drent stood and showed the people his life on the coast. He walked away towards the sea, dug in the sand, produced shells, waded into the sea , raised an arm in a spearing action, returned, peals of laughter overcame him. He walked to the edge of the trees; he pointed into the forest, to their tops and then walked back to the beach to where two coconuts lay. They had sprouted where they had landed and he pointed to the ocean. Time passed, Drent chattered and explained. He picked up a stick and brandished it in a warlike fashion. He swept his arm from the ocean to the forest. Dangers in all directions. He finished, walked to the fire, stretched his arms out, turned, walked through the people and into the forest.

There was movement as the tribe went to their shelters for the night. The fire died, the last embers glowed. Plin, Tub and Grith were the last to leave after a deep conversation. The sound of the waves and a gentle breeze guarded the night.

The sun rose, the insects shrilled in the bush, swallows swooped across the beach, sailing the wind. Drent stood knee deep in the sea. A deep melodious sound escaped him, the people moved to the entrances of their shelters to see Drent beckoning them out. It was time to start learning, to start exploring, to be aware of the dangers that lay ahead. And so Drent started to teach and instruct the tribe in his ways. The men grumbled, the women were eager.

The men waded into the sea, fish were caught. The women moved into the forest, they gathered berries and fruit. Drent was everywhere, laughing, encouraging, goading.

Days, weeks, months passed. The skills were learnt, slowly. Their new world was hemmed in by the forest and sea; there were mutterings about the need for space. It was unlike their old home where distances went on, but maybe the sea would fill this longing once canoes were built.

The seasons changed. Drent took a party of men up the waterways which sliced through the forest. It was wild country. Hills started to appear, there was the sound of rushing water. The men paddled harder to hold their own against the rapids. Drent stood at the front of the canoe, pointing. The men gazed into the forest. The trees were heavy with fruit. They drove the canoe on to a sandy beach. Drent led them into the forest. A short distance from the river, Drent stood waiting for them to catch up. He stood, not a word, he waited for reaction. He looked at the faces, he heard the grumbles. Then they started to look at the forest and slowly their curiosity encouraged them to explore.

Among the trees and rising into the hills were terraces, now abandoned.

"These were the gardens of my tribe. We had everything we needed to survive; the fish in the sea and now you see the gardens. You must start them again." Drent led them through the terraces. He talked, he did not stop. Did they understand? He handled plants. He showed them fruits. He tore at fruit and ate.

The men returned to the terraces, and this time with a group of women. The work started on renewing. At last the men were eager to accomplish.

14

The seasons passed, contact was made with other tribes who lived deep in the forest. Trade was started. Drent was always there, still he taught and reassured. He often left for days or weeks when the tribe had learnt. He never said where he was going; he had a need to travel.

He took with him tools to make fire, some food until he found more, and a bark cloth to cover him at night. He wanted to be in the forest, he wanted to be on the sea. Drent, they relied on him and now he was less and less near the village.

One evening a canoe crashed over the outer reef. Plin saw it first and walked to the water, he signalled to Tub to join him. They slid a canoe into the water and paddled out. They got nearer and looked. Drent was lashed to the side of the canoe, ropes biting into his limbs. His head was attached to the front. They guided the canoe to the shallows and removed the severed body. Tears flowed as they carried him up the beach. Plin and Tub didn't speak. They burnt him that night, the flames leaping into the sky. The people said they could hear his voice among the trees.

Plin walked to the sea, he stood at the edge and looked out. His shoulders slumped and he wept. Grith went to him and embraced him. After minutes they returned to the others. Plin then turned and faced the sea.

"You fucking bastards, fuck you!"

The words carried across the lagoon to the open sea. Plin then walked to his shelter and threw himself down. They could hear his sobs through the night.

The year rounded in the settlement, they travelled to the terraces, and they tended the old sites. They became confident, there was a belonging. Drent's memory was kept alive; they were always talking about him. They felt his presence in the forests, on the sea, up the rivers. Other tribes visited. Plin questioned them about Drent's death.

Plin left the settlement suddenly one day. With a few possessions, he walked to the sea, followed by the tribe. There were farewells, he went among the people, touching. Grith and Tub held him close, he smiled, he spoke. Finally he put his possessions into a canoe and pushed off into the lagoon and towards the reef. Arms were raised in farewell; there were shouts of support as he paddled away through the reef and around the headland.

He was gone.

15

Plin was paddling on a sparkling sea, now far from the settlement. He kept near the coast. His skin glistened in the sun as he struck the water with his paddle. He spent many days at sea, going to land at night to sleep and eat. He caught fish and picked the fruit in the forest. He found a river mouth and started inland. It was a wide river, the forest hugged the banks. After an hour on the river he saw a village. Plin made for the bank of the river and hid among the reeds. New people, he had to be careful.

He looked and saw men of different skin colour, different clothes. He waited until darkness; the last rays of the sun streaked the river. He made his move, and slowly glided across the river to a landing area. He ran the canoe on to the sand.

He walked towards the village and found himself among people of his own kind. They were sitting in lines and tied together. They didn't look up as Plin approached. He moved to a rough shelter and looked through a gap and saw men drinking, talking, laughing, their skins were pale, their bodies covered in clothes. Plin looked at each man in turn and saw that the man in the centre of the shelter was wearing the necklace that Drent used to wear. Plin was filled with anger when he saw the necklace, but he must not give away his presence. There was time to think and decide what to do.

He returned the way he had come, passed the people. He stopped, returned to the people, and started to remove the ropes from their wrists and legs. He had to hurry. They moved silently into the forest and darkness. Plin returned to his canoe, crossed the river, and waited for daylight.

As the light lifted into the sky, there was noise and movement in the village. There were shouts; they must have found the people gone. Plin was awake and a smile covered his face at the thought. He couldn't move from his hiding place for fear of being seen.

Plin waited all day, and as darkness came he paddled away. He had to carry the news and warn of these new people. He had to return to Tub, Grith and the others. It would take him days but the urgency was great. What was happening in the land? Plin sensed danger and terrible changes. His efforts took him within a day of his people. He came ashore, set up a small shelter, to rest and eat. He lay looking out to sea, he was tired, the light was slowly fading, the waves gently lapped on the beach. Plin was suddenly on his feet. In the far distance, on the horizon, he saw a strange object. He walked to the edge of the water. It was a ship, but not one that Plin had ever seen before. The ship moved closer to the land. Plin heard a clattering across the sea. The ship stopped.

Plin had to sleep and then leave at the first signs of dawn. He moved into the forest and dragged the canoe further up the beach. He looked out towards the ship and saw pin pricks of light.

Plin left before light. He had only hours to go before safety and friends. He arrived at the village in the early afternoon. The children saw him first coming through the reef. They scampered to the shelters to pass the news to the adults and soon there was a crowd on the beach. Many of them waded out to Plin and rushed the canoe on to the sand. They surrounded him, touched him, greeted him. Tub and Grith moved through the throng, they took hold of Plin and welcomed him home.

The tribe gathered in the evening in front of their shelters. They had come from the terraces, the forest, the sea. A fire was lit, and food was passed around. Plin arrived; excitement and fear gripped the people.

Plin spoke, "I went to look for the people who killed Drent. Drent showed us how to live by the sea, how to use the forests and how to work the terraces. He introduced us to other peoples. We now have everything we need, we share our food, we trade with other tribes, but there is change coming, and I think it might be terrible. I travelled up the coast and up a river. I saw different people. I saw the man who killed Drent. I was afraid and I decided to return. On my way back I saw a boat out to sea, another sign of change. We must go out on the tracks and spread the news. We must warn people"

Plin continued speaking, the night drew in. The fire was embers by the time he had finished. The people were in no doubt as to what had to be done. They discussed into the night and finally there was agreement. Who was to stay and who was to go out and spread the news was decided. Plin was to lead a group to where the track divided and then they would go separate ways.

Those chosen to warn left in the early morning light before the village was awake. They all carried small bundles, supplies to see them through the days ahead. They hurried. They took the track to the terraces where they split up. Plin had the furthest to journey. There were goodbyes and touching where four tracks met. Some of them would stay together until other tracks appeared but soon they were on their own and heading to the interior. Plin was on a path that stayed near to the sea before it turned inland. He knew many of the places he passed. He came to a lookout and stared out to sea.

Whales were moving down the coast, their migration had started. He then turned and walked inland along a well-worn track into the forest. There were signs of unusual disturbance on the track. There were strange foot marks. He had to hurry on; maybe he was already too late.

Two days of walking brought Plin to the edge of the forest and the start of the barren regions. He had met nobody; he knew that there was a settlement near. He gained height and reached a rocky outcrop. He stopped and looked. The settlement was far below. He watched from a hidden place. There was no movement. Plin descended and entered the area of scattered shelters. No one. A fire was smoking in a compound. Only the sound of birds, otherwise silence. He went from shelter to shelter.

He moved out of the area and settled himself among a stand of trees to wait. He saw a woman moving slowly below the escarpment where Plin had been. He walked towards her, and as he got closer he saw the despair on her face. She beckoned and he followed her to a shallow lake set among stunted bushes. The scene stunned Plin: first no one, but then everyone. They had been hacked and mutilated. There was no life. Plin turned from the horror, he went to the woman. She was mute. She pointed down a track and then walked away. Dusk was falling. It was too dangerous to travel at night. Plin moved away from the settlement and the massacre to find a place to rest for the night. He found a safe hideaway, it wasn't perfect. He ate and then lay down to sleep. His mind turned on the day's events.

Daylight came early, the cackle of birds, the strumming of insects charged Plin into action. He went to look for water.

He knew where to find it among the stunted bushes and plants, a quick meal and then he was on his way, gliding over the country. To warn and to find those responsible for the massacre. The afternoon approached, it was a silent time in the bush. Plin had heard the old people say that the afternoon was when the spirits walked the land.

Plin was upon them. In front he saw a large group of men walking slowly. The same kind of men he saw at the river. This time they had animals with them, animals that Plin had never seen before. They were carrying packs and in front of them women of his kind, tied together.

He followed them through the afternoon until they stopped for the night. Plin disappeared into the shadows, to wait and watch. A fire being lit, cooking smells, and later the screams of the women. Silence eventually fell on the camp. Plin decided to journey on and warn those in their path.

He travelled during the night. He knew the paths. He had travelled these paths as a boy with his father and mother many years ago. He remembered his father teaching him about the land, the places to find water and food. He knew of settlements nearby, he would make for them.

Plin was tired, he had to rest. He could see the first signs of dawn. He found a place in the trees but he was soon on his way again.

In the middle of the day he reached his destination. A village hidden in the rocks off the main path. As he got nearer he sensed silence. There was no life. He slowly approached. The people had left. Maybe they already knew, they had been warned. Plin decided to wait. The strangers had to be near. He found a high place where he would wait and watch.

Hours passed, the day grew late and then he saw a large gathering approaching on the path. The animals, the tied women and the strangers. Plin retreated into the rocks and bushes. They got ready for the night. Plin's gaze was drawn to the same man wearing Drent's necklace. He would choose his moment.

16

Plin returned to the sea. He felt powerless about what was happening around him. Ships were arriving, many people of other tribes were taken, some to the ships, never to be seen again.

Plin, Tub and Grith were together again with the people of the village. They were still safe. Plin gathered the people together, they had to talk. They could stay or move on. To be found and suffer the same fate as others. Their old life was fading, the certainties were shifting. Life used to be easy. There was plenty, they could move and roam as they wanted, but now life was restricted. Once they spoke to other tribes and news was plentiful; it was dangerous to move from the villages and travel over the land now. Movement was what they yearned for most, they were even afraid to work the terraces or move along the coast. The children would not learn from their parents if they couldn't travel. There would be lack of food if they didn't go to the terraces or go to sea. Plin, Tub and Grith had to think of a new way. Soon they would be found if they didn't leave. They might have to move to the margins. This was where they could survive and not the strangers.

Ships were still arriving, ports were being built. The strangers were moving inland. Land was being cleared. There was no care in the way they treated the land. The people they met had been brutally treated.

The tribe was on the move again. They went inland to the deserts to survive. They knew the deserts, life was difficult but they had lived there before and had flourished.

Their movement was detected by the strangers. They moved quickly from the coast, through the giant trees of the forests into the rocky areas and finally to the sand and scrub. They were being followed. Plin could see the followers far behind. A group of men with animals. Plin held back to watch them. The sun beat down. Soon the tribe were far ahead. They halted and Plin and Tub started back to locate them.

They walked for hours and came to an area of low scrub. In front of them were the followers. They were lying on the ground, the animals scattered. Plin and Tub walked among them. They were gasping for breath. Their water gone. The sun had attacked their exposed skin and they begged for shade and water. Plin and Tub turned their backs on them and walked into the land, away.

Plin and Tub returned to the tribe, they seemed listless. These were people who were being hunted, pursued. They had to move constantly. They were used to being on the move but not the pursuit. It had made them wary of other people, where once there was sharing, now there was grabbing and hoarding. Lives were changing; the years of plenty were disappearing. Plin was becoming isolated from the tribe. He was constantly thinking of how to deal with the new circumstances. He felt at a loss. Where should they move to? The pursuers were dead, there must be others. They couldn't move further into the interior, even they would find living difficult.

Plin spoke to the tribe "We must find a way to live our old lives. There are places in the deserts, on the coast where we won't be found. Tub and I found them when we wandered the land. We have been chased for too long now, so we will move to a hidden place and if they find us we will make a stand. I know a place with plenty of food and water but we have to start as soon as we can. We'll stay here for the night and start early."

The dawn broke and the tribe had already been walking for several hours. Plin walked ahead watching the land for strangers. They went into mountainous country covered by dense forest. The path was clear, used for centuries by people moving to other parts, the lifelines. The forest was alive with birds and skittering animals. The path was narrow; the tribe were strung out in a long line.

It took three days to reach the hidden place. They were tired but welcomed the chance to stop and explore their new surroundings. They were hidden by the forest and the mountains but they feared discovery, and discovery was what the strangers were planning, not only for Plin, Tub and Grith but for all the people of the land.

17

The burning started, black smoke swirled into the clear sky blocking the sun, and blue became grey. The smoke found its way down the valleys, into the rivers. The people choked and moved to higher ground, but the smoke surrounded them. There was movement in the forest and among the rocks, the sound of voices and animals. Birds screeched through the trees trying to get away from the leaping flames and thick dancing smoke. The people scattered, they were overcome by the wall of heat. Plin yelled trying to keep them together, but it was of no use. He ran for his life, stumbling and leaping through the trees, across the rocks, towards the river. He jumped into the river, the flames lapped around him.

He allowed the current to carry him down the river, crashing against rocks, tumbling over rapids, until he left the burning land behind. He washed up on a small beach. Exhaustion: he crawled from the beach to the undergrowth and slept.

He woke during the night. The smell of the smoke had gone, stars filled the sky. The landscape was silent. He started to retrace his flight. He arrived at the burnt landscape.

Plin walked through the ashes. He came across the burnt remains of his people. They were lying in clusters. He stopped and stood in the waste land. He screamed and tears flowed. Everybody was gone. Wisps of smoke still rose like his departed people surrounding him. He was crushed by his grief. Then he started to walk away from the destruction. He walked through the rocks, the broken land and out into the desert. He would have to survive here, it would be difficult, but he knew the ways.

18

I looked up and towards Raimund; he was still looking into the distance. I then saw my Aboriginal friends moving down through the boulders and bush. How long had we been like this? Raimund approached me. I had many questions to ask him. He put out his hands and pulled me to my feet. We stood staring at each other.

"Jack you don't need an explanation, why should we always be looking for a meaning and have everything explained? It is for you to think it through, come to your own conclusions."

The four of us returned to the shack. It took several days. We didn't talk about what each of us had been through. We slept in the open and spoke about the many things we encountered on the way. Raimund stayed on for a few days. Jim and Sam returned to their home.

I saw Raimund off at Perth airport. I felt a lasting bond

with him. We embraced, tears in our eyes. He was returning to Colombia.

"Jack, I will see you in my home next time, don't be long in coming. I have lots to show you and lots to talk about." I laughed and watched him weave his way through the crowds to the departure gate and just as he was moving out of sight he turned and shouted, "There is an island in the south seas, it's called – "

The name of the island was swallowed by the airport din. He disappeared.

19

I didn't hear from Raimund for several years and in that time the shack was raised on poles with a perfect view of the ocean. Jessica and I raised a family, Carla, Samantha and Oliver. The ocean was my life, and although I still fished it, I became more and more involved in its preservation.

Sitting looking out to the ocean, I started to read Dad's journals. His immaculate hand writing made it a pleasure to read. It was about the time when he arrived from Ireland. I always loved the description of his first days and then his life brought together in a few paragraphs. I found it strange that he referred to himself in the third person in some of the manuscript. I often wondered why.

The immigrants poured off the ship. A new land, a new life. They had left behind their countries, reeling from hardship and despair. A continent broken by nationalism. Now hope was beckoning. They crowded the dockside to obtain in their passports that stamp, 'Landed Immigrant'. Then out into the sparkling sunshine to be greeted by relatives or friends, who had already made the decision and had the courage to start a new life.

Italians ,Yugoslavs, Greeks, English, Irish, and many others bustled on the quay, waiting for their transport to the city. Friendships made on the ship were now at an end as people went their different ways. Some were hurried away by relatives and friends, the others, who had nobody waiting for them were directed to buses and taxis. They would be taken to hostels and boarding houses. As they set off, they peered out at a strange alien world. The light was extreme, the heat suffocating, the vegetation extraordinary, and then the city, but first the suburbs, sprawling. The bus entered a compound with huts stretching into the distance. This was where the families were to be housed temporarily. Did they wish they were back in the verdant countryside of Ireland or the sparkling mountains of Greece?

The bus stopped, the families got off, and now the leftovers remained to be transported to homes which took in single souls. Christy was nervous, who was he going to find at the family he was allotted to? Would they be welcoming after the long sea voyage? The need to work, money was tight. Many had gone before him and had made a life, different, but that was the reason they were making changes. The bus stopped outside a clapboard house. His name was called, he shuffled down the aisle with his possessions, one bag. He thanked the driver, walked up to the door of the house and knocked. An elderly, sun burnt man opened the door. He was welcomed in. A woman appeared from the shadows. He was shown to his room which looked out on a veranda at the back of the house. A parrot was eyeing him from its stand.

The adjustments, he expected them. The shadow had lifted. He thought back to Ireland, of landlords, of backbreaking work to put money into his pocket, of smothering deference, where everybody knew their place, would he find the same here?

They were a kind couple, the house was friendly. The man spoke of his knowledge of the country and urged Christy to find work out of the city. After a week he left. He took a bus early one morning, north. He had been told of jobs in a town on the coast, it was hundreds of miles away. The journey took hours, even overnight. He watched the countryside, the small towns out of the window. It was hot. It couldn't be more different to Ireland. Eventually the town. The sea dazzled as he walked to the beach, fishing boats were lined up beside a quay. No more than a few hours after arriving in the town, Christy had been signed on as crew on one of the boats.

A feeling of satisfaction swept over him when the boat glided out into the ocean. He had been shown what to do, a simple job, but he would work his way up. Christy looked back at the land. It stretched into the distance. It was his land now and he would get to know it. He would learn from it. He would learn from the first people as well as those who had made his journey. He had an immense sense of excitement being on the edge of discovery.

Christy fished, worked the land, ran the local store, explored the vast hinterland, became well known for his knowledge. Had it all been worth it? There was no doubt in his mind; it had been a terrific journey. He remembered his first steps, maybe too much optimism at first, but that is how it should have been. Welcome to the land.

I closed the journal and thought about what had happened since.

And what of me and Mum? After Dad's time on the coast, he bought a roadhouse on the highway heading north. It was where I grew up. He married Mum a year after he arrived in Australia, she came from The Pilbara. I was an only child and was loved intensely by them.

The roadhouse was a fuel stop, eating place, a place to

stay, camping and caravan park. When he bought it, there was a store and fuel pump, nothing else. After a few years it was well known to travellers on their way north or south. It was Christy's Place. He employed the local mob to run the camping ground and the shop, and it was deeply significant as a bridge between the cultures.

Dad was always thankful that he needed so little to lead a happy life, and that seeped through to me. We often visited the coast which was an easy drive and where I learnt about the sea. Mum was an organiser and it was she who had planned the roadhouse and the services we offered. Dad brought with him his love of books and the roadhouse had a room devoted to those books. Travellers could borrow them and you know every single book borrowed, was returned. And that is where I found out.

I found out, we found out. Dad would suddenly pack the car for a night out in the bush, leaving the roadhouse in the hands of Klipo. We drove out, maybe fifty kilometres, set up camp, just to look and listen. We waited for sunrise and bleary eyed, returned. There were no certainties, sometimes after eating lunch, he said, "to the coast!" We set off, wait until sunset and return. Klipo loved our ways, and we loved it when his mob came to the roadhouse.

Travellers joined in the unannounced as the bare bones of the sun's rays sank below the horizon. The mob moved off and the evening silence surrounded us.

After the evening meal, I often walked with Mum along the road to a track, we climbed a low hill which overlooked home and in the distance the sea. The space, the silence welcomed us as friends.

Dad had ideas. The clown convention, that was his best, and together with Mum, whose energy was enormous, they transformed the campsite into a whirlpool of laughter. He displayed the art of the indigenous people, combining it with song and dance.

Mum and Dad were in their seventies, I had left to work on the coast and had found the shack when the ironmen came. They told Dad that he was sitting on a mountain of iron ore and they wanted it. An American with one eye told him this! The road would be redirected and they would build him another roadhouse. Dad didn't want that, his roadhouse was near to sacred sites and he wanted to keep it that way. The courts didn't see it like that, they sided with the ironmen. The land was appropriated, the roadhouse, the valleys, the sacred sites, all plundered.

There is a valley not far away where an old giant Eucalyptus tree grows. Dad loved that valley. He was found dead under the tree, he had died of grief. His funeral was held at the dead of night. A vast column of mourners followed the coffin through the country, led by an Irish band, Klipo out front, to the tree where he was buried. It really was something.

Mum, she lived into her nineties. She set up a foundation to stop people like the ironmen stealing land. It didn't work. She was buried beside Dad. A Eucalyptus sapling was planted beside their graves, to take over from the giant when its time came.

The books that Dad had at the roadhouse, I have them all in the shack now. There is a room out the back where they are filling the shelves. Friends and strangers moving along the beach know of my collection, they borrow and always return. I know many of the books but one day Echo, a tribal elder who had borrowed a book, and when returning it, I noticed the calm and wellbeing on his face. "You must read it Jack, and when you have, come and see me, I'll tell you more."

I was intrigued. The book, no more than a hundred and fifty pages, black and white photographs scattered through it. I settled one afternoon and read. It had been published in 1951 in London, but apart from that there were no clues as to what I was going to encounter.

My name is Trida, I am an Aboriginal woman from The Pilbara and I sailed from Sydney to Europe in 1933 on a cargo ship bound for Rotterdam – "

I read the book in a couple of hours and was astonished by its contents.

I had never been to sea before. I was fearful of how I would be treated on board. I soon fell into a routine. Left to myself I worked hard in the galley preparing the meals for the crew, and was somewhat an object of curiosity. Had they ever seen a black face among the crew and a woman?

The voyage took eight weeks and when she arrived in Rotterdam, Trida made her way to London. It was here that her extraordinary life continued against all the odds. She was hired as crew on a Thames sailing barge. When she was not living on the barge, she rented a room in Limehouse. Well known on the river, and then the landlady of a public house. Her barge days were sporadic at that time ,the skipper Jim was keen to keep her on. She had worked the river for a year and when she left, Jim had a figure head of Trida carved and placed on the bow of the barge.

The public house was my home for five years. It was a refuge for many. People of different races, the crews of ships arriving into the Port of London. When I started as the landlady the pub was avoided and then curiosity took hold. It was crammed every night, workers from the docks, from the city, a meeting place for the unions. Jews from the East End. And then the bombs began to fall.
As I slept one night, my pub was obliterated. It was not my war. I went to the pub a day later, as I got nearer I saw a

vast crowd standing near the wreck, they saw me, they clapped and cheered. I left soon after, just time to see to the formalities of a bombed pub, and I went to Dublin. I walked, walking for six weeks, sleeping in ditches, barns, the friendship of strangers nourished me, I had stones thrown at me, shouted at. A ship across the sea. It was 1940. I found a room in Dun Laoghaire. Having been away for seven years, it was time to go home.

Paying a month's rent, scouting the docks for a ship on which to start my long journey home, it was war time. I did find one eventually, bound for New York. The captain signed me on, this time as a deckhand. I had several weeks before the ship sailed. It had suffered damage in a violent storm on its voyage across The Atlantic. During those weeks I made trips out of the city. There was an encounter I wanted to make. I had carried a companion with me from home. The first installments of Finnegan's Wake, I now wanted to buy the complete work and meet Mr Joyce.

Trida asked about, visited bars, went to the theatres, libraries, museums, nobody could give her information on Mr Joyce. When she was walking back to her room, she saw a crowd in the centre of Dublin. They were carrying Irish flags, a speaker was on a platform. She walked to the edge of the crowd, listened, an elderly man beside her smiled at her and held out his hand.

I spent an evening with this man in a bar. His name was Patrick Flanaghan, an Irish Republican who had spent two years in The Pilbara and had recognised me as a person of those parts. How did he know? He just smiled when I asked him. Mr Joyce now lives in Switzerland, and occasionally visits Dublin. Many friends of Patrick's came to the bar that evening, eager to talk to me and hear my story. "Why did you leave your home and come here?" The question was asked many times. "I am interested, just interested." I answered.

Patrick introduced me to his many friends. I was taken to theatres, shown where opposing people clashed, then it was time to leave. I was given a mighty send off the night before sailing and was given a copy of Finnegan's Wake, folded inside a letter signed by everybody there that evening.

I sailed for New York. It took ten days. After the welcome in Dublin I think deeply about how I was treated aboard that ship.

She kept to herself, did the work, the aggressive looks, the profanities wore her down. She didn't go on deck for fear of being thrown overboard.

The ten days on the ship were the unhappiest I spent in the seven years of my odyssey. I often think back on that time and try to understand. I have no easy explanations, I was different, I was discarded as a person.

New York, a cheap hotel, count my money. I had read about a man who had crossed America by stowing away on freight trains. I would do it that way. I wanted to see the city. I listened outside the jazz clubs in Harlem. I met a Sioux man selling trinkets in the street. Poor, dishevelled, yes. I know how you feel, I have experienced the same myself. I went to Ellis Island and imagined the throngs arriving from other lands, a better life?

The war was raging in Europe. I wanted to get away as far as possible, searching the rail yards, listening for a hint, a west bound freight. The information came quite by chance. Leaving my hotel, walking to the freight yards, and seeing a group of rail men, I fell in behind them. They went to a diner. I sat at a table near them, listening. Their destination, Chicago.

Trida crossed America, stowing away, from one train to

another, meeting others, learning of lives, of hardship, making friends in the confines of a freight wagon, saying goodbye to those friends, living on her wits she arrived in San Francisco.

I crossed America on the freight trains, chased by police in railway sidings, heaving myself up on to the wagons, bunking down with hobos, isn't that what they are called? The railway police always two steps behind, fooled at every turn. The wagon door open as I crossed the great plains, traversed the mountains. Waving to those watching the train go passed, they waved back. The fresh air rushing against my face, ruffling my hair. A smile as broad as the plains covering my face. Homesteads far in the distance, Indian reservations, yes, fucking reservations, when they should be on the grasslands. The stories told on that trip, people searching for work, chased off land, setting up shelters by the side of roads and the railroad.

The smoke stack, the smell of coal, even in my wagon, way down the train. At last after days, turning to weeks, the coast. How many trains had I jumped? Dozens. Jackson, a hobo I had met many times on my journey, destined to become a great writer, Orville a great artist. I missed the sound of the tracks, the freedom, the laughing as I fled the police. Sharing the caboose with a friendly train worker. Riding on top of a wagon before being spotted .

I was sad when I had my last sight of a giant locomotive leaving San Francisco as I headed for the ships. Was that Jackson I saw in a crowd as I walked? Keep the books coming, blow open the myths, tell it as it should be told. Goodbye America.

Another cargo ship, crossing The Pacific. What a contrast to the Atlantic crossing. A New Zealand ship, the crew Maoris. Three weeks singing our way to Sydney. Hawaii and Auckland on the way. I couldn't wait for my homeland.

Trida made it home in early 1941. There was more, much more in the book. I leave it to others to read. The deep feelings she had, the love for the pub in Limehouse, the barges plying The Thames, the horror of the coming war. She writes of the English countryside, soon to change for ever.

The Dubliners, her attempt to find James Joyce, only to find that he had died soon after she returned home. There is a picture of Trida in the book, dressed in dungarees outside the pub, by her side, a little boy. The caption reads, "Me and Sam, two days before he died in a bombing raid." Who was Sam?

I went to see Echo. He lived inland from the shack. I parked at the start of the track that led to his house. He saw me coming and raised his hand in greeting.

"Trida was my mother. I had always known that she had written a book about her time in Europe and beyond. I could never find a copy, but there it was in your shack. I still have the copy of Finnegan's Wake and the letter signed by those at her leaving party. I recognise some of those names, writers and poets of the day, isn't that wonderful? Mum died ten years ago."

I asked Echo about Sam in the photograph. "He was an orphan who Mum had taken in and would have brought him back to Australia if he had lived."

I wanted to read the diary that Raimund had left, along with the papers on his first night in the shack. I hadn't buried the diary with the papers, I know I should have. It had been on a shelf all that time .I took it down. Settling back in the chair, I flicked through it. It was in Spanish except for one long section towards the end. I started to read.

13th November 1978.

We went deep into the interior, my friends Antoni and Alfonse, the owners of the riverboat which we were on, had plied the river for many years, transporting goods to the villages strung out along the banks. We had many miles to travel, stopping at night and going on short excursions into the forest. Antoni was an expert on identifying the wildlife, which was all around. He knew where to find exotic and strange creatures which came out when the darkness fell. On the fourth night we stopped at a jetty that jutted out into the river. It led to a house where a friend of mine Sarah lived. She had lived for many years in the forest, escaping. I don't know what from, but she always appeared happy out here in such an isolated place.

In the living room of her house was a grand piano and that evening after the meal, she played. It was an extraordinary performance. Surrounded by the darkness, the night sounds. She played the Rhapsody and many other works. It was an experience I won't forget.

When she had finished and without a word, she rose from her chair, and hugged us each in turn. She disappeared and we sat in silence. We slept long and deeply and in the morning came down to a table laden with local produce. We didn't see Sarah before we left, Antoni told me she went out in the early morning to meet the Jaguars.

Continuing our journey, passing through untouched forest, volcanoes far in the distance, some had plumes of smoke coming from them. We reached our destination after six days. The boat was to be our base. Xlia met us, it was wonderful to see her, she looked as intriguing as ever, we embraced and held each other for minutes.

We started our trek into the highlands. The grasslands, the forest beyond, the mountains in the distance. The first sounds of chainsaws, at first far off and then slowly becoming louder as we got nearer to the trees. Small animals dashed from the cover looking for safety and then larger animals. Tribal people fleeing. The saws were almost upon us. They ceased, the noise of burning wood, sparks and crackling, flames tearing through the downed trees. Bleeding stumps standing as memorials to the carnage. Gunfire heaped on the people refusing to leave. Animals forced into dead ends and then massacred. Vast crawlers tearing at the forest. Insects in flight, butterflies too slow in their escape devoured by flames, dying at our feet. Men tramping forward, chainsaws slung over their shoulders like modern day spears. Men shouting.

The crawlers advancing, squeezing the life blood out of the earth, the microbes crushed under their tracks. The insects screaming. Giants of the forest felled in minutes, hundreds of years wiped out. I ran forward, trying to protect a giant tree, then I thought I was gone. I had put myself in mortal danger, I was angry. I was being pushed and shoved by a brute of a man with an axe, the overseer. "Fuck off Roello and take that Indian bitch with you." His face a mask of hate. I was petrified by this man's indifference to the forest, people and the animals.

I retreated to a high place, looked towards the volcanoes. The largest one was roaring with grief as the destruction continued, sending boulders skyward, a plume of smoke spreading over the country.

I fled with Antonio and Alfonse back to the river. It took us several hours. I had seen what I had been told by others. Sadness gripped me, the horror of it. On our way back to the city, we visited Zania on the chocolate farm. The gentleness of her surroundings and her occupation was cathartic after witnessing such destruction. I returned to my home, I felt safe, a home which I had converted from an old printing works. It took many months to convert. The vast views over the city to the Pacific was the reward. Arriving and walking up the shallow stairs to my bedroom, pictures of indigenous people watching me, I knew I was home.

The entry finished, but just as I was closing the diary, and putting it on the table in front of me, I saw another passage in English

I was the president of a country in South America, it started to prosper for the poor, there was no idealism, haven't we had enough of that, leaders ushering in a new dawn, only for it to end in brutish behaviour. I was overthrown with the connivance of The United States, my presidency lasted eight months. You will find no mention of it anywhere. Why was that? Corporations wanted to dominate the country and search for our resources. I fled and have been hunted ever since. My mother was Irish you know, she taught me to think beyond. She said that curiosity and imagination are the king and queen of humanity. To applaud difference. Look beyond the nonsense fed to us . As I left my country by air, I looked down and saw the lights go out all over the city. What are leaders afraid of. Do you know what Tom Paine said?

He said, "If there must be trouble, let it be in my day, that my child may have peace."

Who did he say this to? It appeared to be a conversation he had written down, so as to remember it. I was intrigued.

In the back cover of the diary was a pocket where diarists often store letters or scraps they have kept. This pocket contained a letter of six typed pages. I felt I was intruding, but I wanted to know more. It was dated the 4th May 1971.

My dear Raimund,

It is now some years since I have written to you and in that time I have lived in London, Prague and have visited Japan. From the address on this letter you can see that I am now living in Ethiopia. Yes, a woman in Ethiopia working as a surgeon. It has raised eyes but I am accepted by the medical profession here, and I plan to stay. More about that later. I always remember your love for the country although you stayed for a very short time, two months, wasn't it? I have been here for six years now. And I remember your fascination with the Ethiopian philosopher as you called her. I once met her and felt there was something very other worldly about her, which there was, but what I remember mostly about her was her ability to assimilate with other cultures, religions, and races. In such a conservative society that is not easy. I married five years ago, my husband is a tribal elder, who I met when on a tour of villages dispensing medicines and dealing with shocking injuries and diseases. I now have a son of four and a daughter of six.

I truly wish we could meet again, but knowing of your nomadic lifestyle and your need to keep to the shadows to avoid governments of certain persuasions, this will not be easy. When I last saw you I was on my way to London, where I stayed for three years. It was a wonderful city, but it wasn't for me. I tried to make friends. Apart from those I worked with closely, I found it very difficult. Being a tribal woman from The Amazon brought forth scorn and laughter from many. Ask your wife Xlia! And then Prague.

As a woman from The Amazon living in Prague was an astonishing experience. They were fascinated by me I had been warned by friends that winter fell hard in the city. It certainly was cold. My stay, and I was there for a year, was one of exceptional curiosity and love from the people I met. Working in children's wards in the hospital brought me into close contact with families, who had never met a foreigner before and certainly not one like me! I even managed the language.

I met Vaclav Havel, who at that time was very bothersome to the government, what a great man. I asked him to come to The Amazon and meet my people one day. He said he would but events overtook the invitation. I made friends with a Japanese doctor. He worked in the same hospital and said to me, when he left to return to Japan, that I must visit him in his small town outside Tokyo and I did.

I went to Moscow and took the Trans Siberian train to Vladivostok and then a ship to Yokohama . The country I arrived in was very strange to me and I was subjected to stares wherever I went. I turned this to my advantage and found that welcoming these stares was the way to meet and communicate with people. Mitsu, the Japanese doctor, met me in the ryokan where I was staying in Tokyo. If you ever go to Japan experience these inns. They are simple, and places of peace and calm. I was in Japan for six weeks. Mitsu took time off work to travel with me. The most profound time was a visit to Hiroshima, and a stay in the mountains in a town where a revered Zen monk used to live. Your visit to South East Asia came to mind when I was in the mountains.

Hiroshima, what can you say that hasn't already been said, and I know that you have written about it in some of your books. I laid a small stone, that I had brought from the Amazon, on a cairn near the site of the catastrophe. I wonder if it is still there?

Mitsu said goodbye to me as I set out for India and the Middle East. I had booked my passage on a freighter, which was destined for Marseilles. I had been told that it would be a six week voyage. I was excited by the idea, the ports we would visit and the knowledge that I would gain. It is always sad when you leave a good friend like Mitsu. He remained on the quayside waving until the distance swallowed him up. My tears flowed. I probably would never see him again.

The crew of the freighter were from Goa, the captain and officers Greek. They were such a mix and I felt entirely at ease. There were two other passengers, a man in his eighties, who was from New York, and a young man from Sweden. We were an odd trio, but even so, we laughed, discussed and argued our way. At the ports where we stopped, and we stopped for days sometimes, we would go together into the cities. Then there were just two of us, me and Erik the Swedish man. The American, Ernie, did not appear back at the ship when we were due to leave. This was in Bombay. The Greek captain shrugged his shoulders and we were on our way. They searched his cabin, he had taken all his belongings. I would love to know where he went, and what he is doing now. He told me about his life and about his home in New York. If I am ever that way, I will go to his home. I have every confidence in his welfare . I often think that my friends and family feel the same about me, the warmth it gives me urges me on.

My final port was Haifa and from there I went to Crete. I suppose it was a pilgrimage, to lay some flowers on the grave of Nikos Kazantzakis in Heraklion. Please read Zorba the Greek, there is a very short passage in the book that has remained with me through the years.

I had no intention of going to Ethiopia, but I saw a job vacancy in Addis in a hospital. They were looking for a paediatric surgeon, I applied, got the job, and have made my home here. As I look back over the years I feel an intense feeling of good fortune. It certainly has not all been good, but as I look out over the highlands while writing this letter, I have been very lucky.

It is evening now and I feel a sense of loss and loneliness. I am far away from my first home, the small village in the Amazon forests. I miss it, my family, and friends. I have travelled so far physically and in my mind, that I wonder if I will ever be able to go back. My children, my husband, will they want to travel with me to where I started? This is what is troubling me. My happiness here has been more than I could have expected, but a moment has arrived within me, a yearning for that dark river, the village, the towns, my people. Will they welcome me back or am I now too far along another path?

The time has come to talk to Lanca, my husband, about this. He is a most honourable man. I said that he was a tribal elder, but he is much more. His dedication to the people is quite without fault. He has supported them through quarrels with the central authorities. He has been detained for weeks, for speaking up about their entitlements, usually land ownership, to a point where the threats have worn him down. This has affected me, and of course the children. What would he think if I suggested to him that we go to South America? The leap in culture would be enormous for him and the children. I have been told there is an Ethiopian restaurant in Iceland!

He is away for a few nights with the children, visiting relatives in the north, so I have the days to think how I will approach this dilemma. You have been a huge influence in my life Raimund, ever since you met my brother Pran, going into the forest with him, hearing the music being played, and then the destruction. Pran writes to me often. He is my connection now with my homeland. There are forces now so hostile to his attempts to preserve and protect the people and the forest that I worry for his life

Before I finish this letter, I must tell you about my journey from Crete to Ethiopia, which was first of course by sea to Egypt and then on. I travelled The Nile with the assistance and kindness of the local people I met. First let me tell you about Khan. He was a ferryman on The Nile who transported goods and people far into the interior of Egypt. Meeting him in a café in Cairo was a stroke of luck. He was sitting at the next table with his family, and we fell into conversation, with difficulty, in English. I told him I was on my way to Ethiopia and could he help with my plans. His felucca was leaving in two days, it had room on board for me. Knowing my wish to travel overland, he said that he would introduce me to Omar, who plied his trade between The Nile, through Sudan to the border with Ethiopia. What drew me to this offer was that I would be travelling with a camel caravan through the deserts. Khan needed to see that Omar would take a foreigner and a woman. He wouldn't know until reaching the last port on his part of The Nile.

My accommodation on the felucca was sparse. It was thronged by passengers returning to their villages. I was quite a curiosity, but I was met with warmth by these strangers who included me in their gatherings as we sailed south.

My memories, and there were many on the voyage. The pastoral endeavours along the banks, the towns we stopped at, the villages we passed. The routines and patterns of life were everywhere you looked. The felucca carried me to the final destination where I said goodbye to Khan, but before doing so, he disappeared into the crowds at the jetty and came back with Omar.

I had been nervous about meeting Omar, I needn't have been, he welcomed me most graciously. He was a giant of a man. He said "Of course you are welcome." Offering me his hand and speaking in what I thought was perfect English.

The journey started, fifty camels, Omar leading, me close behind on what he called his quietest and calmest camel. A scene that hadn't changed for hundreds if not thousands of years. Omar used to fall back and ride by my side. He talked of the traditions of the caravans, the goods they carried, the men he employed, the landscapes we passed through, and our destination in the Abyssinian Hills, weeks away. We settled into a routine, long days, preparing food, setting camp for the night. I helped where I was needed, always conscious of who I was. I tried to speak the dialect much to their amusement. The long days of moving across the desert remains vividly in my mind. The landscape dwarfed us, the dunes, the emptiness, the silence. When we stopped for the night and were setting up the camp, the men were very concerned for my modesty, and we laughed a lot about this. The caravan stopped at an oasis occasionally, water was taken on, food was bought, friends greeted. I was introduced, and after suspicions were peeled away, I was treated as an honoured guest. The sharing of provisions gladdened me

After a week, we entered Omar's village. There were about a dozen houses. "This is my home." It was at the edge of an oasis, a green island among the harsh sand. Goats came out to greet us, followed by children and then the women. We stayed for two days. Omar told me that I must be a guest in his home. I slept a lot over the days and consumed what was incomparable honey and yoghurt. His wife made me welcome as did his two children. Then the caravan was on its way. The night before we left, music filled the desert night when one of the camel drivers and his family performed for us, to wish us luck on the next stage of the journey.

There was still a great distance to cover. On the second day out from the village, a sandstorm struck. Omar ordered us to stop and form the camels into a tight circle. Hunkered down we saw out the storm which was vicious. I remember thinking, as the storm battered us, about my Amazon childhood, being surrounded by the animals of the forest, while here in the desert, the distances sometimes filled me with dread. I would often see a lone figure walking from the desert track into the far distance, where there appeared to be nothing. I wondered, where are they going? Then I thought of the lines of connection, they were going home, like I did on the rivers or treading the paths among the trees.

Home.

It was time to say goodbye to Omar and the others, we had reached the border with Ethiopia. Omar had arranged a place for me to stay. We walked down darkened alleyways, when we came to a barrier. There was a sleepy guard in a small wooden shack. Omar coughed to attract his attention, the guard looked up and waved us on. Arriving at a tall building, he pushed the door open and we entered a small courtyard. Although it was late, an elderly man was sitting at a desk near the entrance. He beamed with delight on seeing Omar and held out his hand. Omar said he must go and that onward transport would be here for me in the morning. I couldn't have asked for more, his kindness shone out. He took both my hands in his and wished me a safe journey. I was sad to see him leave. I watched him disappear into the dark street.

I was shown to my room, where I collapsed into an exhausted heap. I lay in bed that night and thought back on my journey with Omar, his men and the camels. There was something about the experience that I couldn't quite explain. I missed the smells, deep antique smells, leather, blankets, spiced foods. The sounds, moving slowly through the landscape, wind, sand being blown, creaking of the harnessing on the camels, shouts of the men, birds flying over. The camels at night, chewing, rumbling stomachs, feeling their presence in the darkness. Lying on my bedding, looking up, the stars stretching forever

Companionship, I hadn't known the camel men long, they had become my companions. I had been welcomed in. They looked after me, I couldn't have asked for more.

Well Raimund, I have written far too much, and it is time for me to sit and think about how I am going to approach Lanca and the move to The Amazon. He is a listener.

When I was waiting for my transport onwards, which wasn't till late afternoon, I decided to go out and walk. I meandered through the streets and entered a square, a beautiful mud daubed building was in front of me. There was an elderly man outside, who, on seeing me, beckoned me over, which surprised me. I walked over, he took me by the arm and guided me up steps, opened a giant door to the building. Mustiness hit me as I went in, books lined the walls. He ushered me through passages and courtyards, chattering away, waving his arms, not a word did I understand, but I didn't need to, his enthusiasm was infectious.

There was a woman sitting in one of the rooms and when we went in, she got up and welcomed us with outstretched arms. On the table where she had been sitting, were paper, pens and an open book. My guide left the room, the woman gestured that I should sit down. I chose a chair near to where she had been writing. She walked over to a glass vessel containing water, poured two glasses, offering me one of the glasses, which I took. When she had sat down, she busied herself with the paper and pens and then turned her chair to face me. What an elegant woman, dressed in blue robes, she must have been in her seventies, clear, sparkling eyes, and so much goodness in her smile. A wild love for all around her.

She offered up her hands and took mine, gently squeezing. Then she got up and walked over to books stacked on a table and said, "Old knowledge passed down to be rediscovered. I live my life in widening circles. I have known this library for years. I come here from my home, travelling on foot. It takes me two weeks, carrying my belongings on my trusted mules. You know they have travelled the path from my home to the library for so long that they can guide me. I love this place, I am surrounded by wisdom and knowledge. It travels back thousands of years, the most profound insights to our existence, but it is lost to the world. Somehow a deep sense of participation must be found."

I stayed with her for several hours, mindful of my onward journey. It was time to leave, she pressed a book into my hands. "My name is Hospadyr, I live near Addis, this is my address, please visit me."

I wish you all the luck with your quest.
From your friend, Stravia.

I looked up and out to sea, taking in what I had read and although there were parts that were distressing, I imagined two people moving through the world, making of it as they thought best, and using that for the good of others.

20

An island in the South Seas. Lucia was the obvious person to ask. I tried to phone her several times, but there was never any answer, so I went to Melbourne. It was the quiet season at work, I had time to spare. Arriving at the bus stop near her house, I saw that the shutters were closed. I went up to the front door and rang the bell. It echoed in the hall. Nobody came to the door. I waited for a few minutes and then turned to leave and as I did so, I saw an elderly lady standing in the road watching me. I went towards her and when I got closer, I recognised Lucia. She had aged in the few months since I had seen her. She grabbed my hands and held them to her face.

"Jack you must come in."

"Why is your home shut up?"

"I've been away. I went to see Raimund. How strange you arrive here on the day I come back." Nothing seemed strange to me about Raimund's story and where it was leading me. We went into the house. It was as I remembered it. Lucia threw open the shutters and the light streamed in.

I felt awkward being there when she had just returned, but Lucia seemed to sense this and said that I was welcome in her house and that I must stay until returning home. I stayed for five days and Lucia told me many things about Raimund, some of which I already knew but a lot was new. I wanted to know where he had gone after leaving Colombia.

"He has many favourite places in the world, Europe, his home in Colombia, here, but when he was travelling as a young man, he found an island in French Polynesia. It was there that he settled for several years and did most of his writing, and that is where he is now. I have been with him for two months. He won't return to Colombia until he feels safe again. Antoni is looking after his house there. I know he told you that he had been a president of a country in South America. Eight months that was all. He led a good government that many others looked upon for guidance. He abolished the armed forces which had been trained by the US. He was trying to break the cycle of violence not only in his country but around the world. The cycle of violence that afflicts us all. He was naïve. He had a great sense of mischief you know. People don't like that."

Lucia showed me pictures of his Pacific island, but would not tell me the name. "When we were children in Argentina, Raimund was fascinated by a shop keeper in our town. His name was Old Hazard; he was one of the original indigenous people of Argentina. We never knew his real name. There was mystery in that shop for children. He sold everything. Medicines, garden implements, tins of food, the daily papers. We even heard that there was a dark room at the back of the shop, but we never saw him selling any cameras or films.

"Old Hazard had been in the town for years, his mother and father had owned the shop before him. We were told that it had the same décor and had never been modernised. He would leave a light on at the back of the shop at night. The window display never changed, dust and cobwebs gathered and when we passed at night, we looked in and shadows cast a flickering story. He lived alone above the shop; we never saw a light on upstairs. There were other mysterious people in town who were friends of Old Hazard but when mother and father talked about them the conversation always returned to Old Hazard. People used to turn to him if they had problems. He had been around so long that people did not remember him ever being young. Had he ever been young, people asked?"

Lucia hesitated while she gathered her thoughts.

"As we grew from childhood, Raimund and I used to wander the countryside, we loved the changing seasons, the animals we saw. During one of our walks, a long way from town, we saw a figure crossing a clearing ahead of us. It was Old Hazard. We had never seen him away from the shop before. We wondered who was looking after it. He was walking away from us and we thought about catching him up, but something told us not to. He disappeared into the trees which closed around him. We started home and were back in town in about an hour and when passing the shop we saw Old Hazard serving customers. It was as if he had been there all the time.

"We returned home and decided the next day to go to where we had seen him in the country. We started early and reached the clearing. We saw Old Hazard walking slowly towards the river where we sometimes went to catch fish. We followed, keeping to the trees and on reaching the river, he was gone. We looked around for many minutes, nothing. Returning to town, and passing the shop, he was there.

"It was months later when we were going to the town that we saw a crowd outside Old Hazards' shop. There was an ambulance. Old Hazard had had a heart attack. After his treatment he went into a home. The shop was closed. For years it remained like that and then one evening Raimund told me that he had been passing the shop and had looked in through the dirty, grimy window and could see a dim light in the back. There was an alley down the side, Raimund went down it and found a door, which he said had been recently used. He listened at the door and he could hear a whirring noise. There was a small window high up to the right of the door and on his tip toes he looked in and saw Old Hazard bending over a tray of liquid, picking it up and tipping it from side to side. Was this the dark room at the back of the shop that we had heard about many years before? What was he doing there? He was meant to be in a home if not dead!

"Raimund returned home and told me what he had seen. The next day while talking to Mother and Father, we mentioned Old Hazard's shop and during that conversation, Mother said that he had died four years ago. Naturally Raimund and I were astonished. That same evening the two of us set out for the shop. When we reached it, we peered through the front window, the light was on, we went to the side door, and looked through the small window. Old Hazard was there. I looked at Raimund and told him I was returning home, this was just too much for me to understand and I was frightened. He said he would stay. I went home.

"After I had gone, he continued to watch Old Hazard. He was producing photographs and he could see that they were ancient scenes. How could this be? While he was distracted for a few moments, Old Hazard appeared at his side in the alley.

"'I knew you would return Raimund, Lucia should have stayed.' Raimund was terrified. 'Come in don't be afraid.' A man who was supposed to be dead. He held out his hand and guided him into the room. We had always remembered Old Hazard as a small frail man, but he towered over

Raimund. He beckoned him over to a table. 'Raimund, you have found out. Come with me, I want to tell you about my life. It was bound to have happened sometime that somebody would find me. I have witnessed some of the most important moments of history, I recorded them in diaries and also sketched them and am now photographing my sketches, look around you. These files contain my work.'

"They walked from room to room which were filled with diaries, boxes of drawings and photographs, all marked with dates. Does it sound familiar Jack? Raimund scanned the shelves, he took down a file, but Old Hazard grabbed his arm. 'Not yet.' They moved into another room where a fire was roaring in the grate. They sat down, Old Hazard offered him a drink which had a taste of something that he could not describe to me, but he said it was sublime. 'Do you remember when you and Lucia saw me in the country? I was on my way to see a friend. His name, well I'll tell you another time.' He then got up and went to a metal box on a shelf; he brought it over to the table. 'Open it Raimund.' He started to open the box, but there was a force holding the lid down. 'Try harder Raimund.' As the lid came off, a light streamed from the inside, dazzling. 'Take a picture out and study it.'"

She stopped and looked at me, as if to check I was still listening. She smiled and continued.

"He removed a picture and stared at it. He never told me what the picture was, it was a defining moment in his life, he has kept the secret ever since. I believe that Old Hazard was and is an enormous influence in Raimund's life. The last time they saw each other was out on the Pampas. They met an elderly lady at an old Estancia, many miles from the city. She was the owner. They went in, the walls were covered with paintings of indigenous people. Raimund felt he recognised some of them. The lady then produced a map and Raimund told me that it was a map the like he had never seen before. The rivers were actually flowing and the forest was moving as if blown by the wind. Raimund has never told me about the conversations he had with Old Hazard and the lady. We never saw Old Hazard again. And the lady's name, that remains a secret. We think that Old Hazard was shot by the regime."

21

We sat quietly after Lucia had told her story, then she said, "You know Raimund faked his death in Rome, he was covering his tracks, they were very near when he fled to Colombia."

"I must see him again Lucia. I still have many things to ask him, I'll travel to the island, if you tell me how and where I can find him." I urged Lucia to tell me.

"All I can tell you is that he is on one of the islands of French Polynesia. You have to go to Tahiti and if you must go I can't stop you. You will have to make contact with a woman who runs a shipping agency. Her name is Mary, she is an islander, she knows everything about the islands. I will give you a letter of introduction. That is all I can tell you. When I was with Raimund he asked after you, he wants to see you again. You must know that many of his friends are being watched and I'm sure you are."

I left Lucia and journeyed back to Perth with the little information I had to find Raimund. Her parting words, "If they find you, at least you don't know his exact location!"

I was sure that Jessica's patience would unravel when I told her about Tahiti, but on telling her, she said, "You must go." I knew I would leave everything in good hands and Joe was equally enthusiastic.

I left in the early spring on a ship out of Sydney to Fiji. I had decided that doing it that way I would have a chance of avoiding followers. It was a cargo ship and I had been told that I could catch other ships if I wanted, as I made my way across the ocean to Tahiti. I watched Sydney Heads disappear as the ship sailed to the Pacific. My feelings were mixed. How long would I be gone? My family, my friends, the business. I had been given a picture of Raimund by Lucia taken in his Pacific home. I displayed it in the cabin along with a picture of Jessica and the children.

I had time to gaze into the vast distances of the ocean. The captain of the ship was a Greek woman from Kalamata in the Peloponnese. She was in her fifties and had been crossing the oceans for thirty years. She said that this voyage was her favourite. There were five other passengers, two Australian couples and a woman from Portugal. The captain, Emeralda, estimated that it would take three to four weeks to reach Tahiti, calling at other islands, loading, unloading. I liked the flexibility of the schedule, the final destination was Chile.

I settled to the days, reading, making friends with the crew, riding on the bridge, exchanging stories of the sea, and then one day having been at sea for a week and after docking at Fiji, I was standing by the rail, looking out , hoping to see whales, I had a feeling of somebody standing beside me. I looked, nobody. I continued gazing. That same feeling I had years ago on the coast of Australia when I was able to see into the past overwhelmed me. I was propelled into the ocean depths. There was no fear, just a feeling of complete tranquillity. Before me was a colossal world, the shoals rubbed against me, the loners welcomed my visit into their domain and suddenly I was on a beach. I was alone wanting Raimund to guide me through this experience. I seemed to feel his presence and he was saying, "This time you can do it on your own Jack, don't be afraid."

I was interrupted in my thoughts by my shipboard

companions. I snapped to the present and followed their gaze and saw two whales leading our ship through the waves. The smile on my face was so wide, it hurt. Nothing else mattered at that moment except those whales crossing that boundless ocean, like the earth travelling through the endless universe.

22

After four weeks I arrived in Tahiti. The others were travelling on to Chile. Emeralda, had become a good friend, and said I must visit her home in Greece one day. I disembarked and walked into the city of Papeete. A shipping agency run by a woman called Mary, there couldn't be many. After booking into a hotel I started asking around. The man in the first agency I visited knew Mary well and directed me to her offices.

She was hesitant in giving me any information but when I spoke of Lucia, she immediately relaxed. We talked about Raimund, but she would not tell me where he was until I gave her the letter of introduction. "I had to be sure you were Jack, the things you have told me about Raimund confirm that. You must come to my house and have a meal and we will talk." A complete sense of relief in having found Mary and that she trusted me.

I went to her house that evening where I was greeted by her husband David. Mary had been delayed. David wanted to know about my voyage from Australia and told me he knew Emeralda. We were sitting on the veranda talking, looking out towards the street, when I saw a car slowly pass, it passed again in the other direction, and I looked at the driver. It was the Talker. The Talker knew that I would lead him to Raimund. I had to change my plans.

Mary arrived and I told her about the Talker. "There is a ship leaving tomorrow for Raimund's island, you will be on that ship and the Talker will have no idea you have left Papeete."

The ship was on its regular tour to the Society Islands group with a doctor on board who tended to the sick and dispensed medicines. It was an overnight journey. I was met by Raimund on the quayside. He looked older but his warmth and humour shone out. His house overlooked a beach where he walked in the mornings and in the afternoon wrote for several hours. I stayed on the island for three weeks. When I first arrived I noticed a photograph, high up on a shelf in the living room and when Raimund was out of the room I took it down and studied it. It worried me. It was a picture of Hitler at one of his rallies. He saw me looking at it and said "We will talk about that later." During those weeks he told me about extraordinary events in his father and mother's lives. We were always out and around the island during the day, and in the evenings the stories.

"My mother was from Ireland, she immigrated to Argentina with her parents in the 1900s. Dad was a Jew from Germany. His father just knew and sensed the atmosphere in Germany and fled with his family. He was a baker and he started a bakery in La Boca in Buenos Aires. It was a very popular venue for the locals. Dad helped in the bakery. He was a good artist. He painted the signs outside the cinemas and Vaudeville theatres, acted in Burlesque shows in his twenties and that is where he met my mother. Mother was a costume designer. His artwork and her costumes were in great demand. They travelled far, even to New Orleans. He had a keen sense of the ridiculous and this attracted the attention of rulers in some countries. He was told to cease upsetting the establishment, he never did. He married mother in 1933, a time when fascism was engulfing Europe. "When he wasn't working in the bakery, he would employ people to help with his paintings and illustrations. His workshop was often raided and the paintings destroyed."

"Life got very difficult for him, the bakery was still going but my grandparents were getting on and the attention from the security men was becoming more and more invasive. Dad and mother had to leave, their lives were threatened. They left on a ship bound for New York and then on to France. He had become a dangerous, divisive person in the eyes of the authorities. His brother and two sisters stayed on and helped with the bakery, but they too were watched, the brother for his writing and the two sisters for organising unions and working among the ragged people. I remember Dad telling me on their departure that his mother looked deeply and questioning into his eyes, no words, "Are you sure you are doing the right thing?"

23

"Roasting coffee, baking bread Jack, some of the best smells in the world. It's late, bed time and let's rise early and walk to the fishing village on the other side of the island."

We set out early with provisions for a long day. The air was clear and still, the morning birds were just waking as we climbed the hill behind Raimund's house and on to the plateau. We stopped at the top and looked out over The Pacific. "You can almost hear God calling," he said, and he was right. Meandering through plantations of coconut, thick forest and into open country. The day was stirring. We sat by a waterfall and then on to the village, arriving at midday, and had our meal with the villagers. Raimund was greeted warmly. Fishermen were returning and we watched them beach their boats and carry their catch to tables on the sand. We retraced our steps in the late afternoon. On reaching the house I saw a light in the kitchen and a figure cooking. Raimund employed a woman from the town to look after the house and to help prepare meals, a feast was waiting for us.

"I didn't tell you why Dad and Mother left South America. Dad had been threatened by the regime in Argentina, and if he continued with his Burlesque routines he would be sent to prison and death would probably follow. He had no alternative. He was in France in 1936 at the time of the Spanish civil war, living in Paris, working as a street artist, not much money doing that. Then he found work in a Burlesque show, a salary which was just enough for survival. They drifted to Spain, meeting many travellers on the way. You know Jack, the great diaspora of the road is despised by the settled. They mixed with Roma, stayed at their camps, adopting some of their customs and crossing The Pyrenees, staying in mountain refuges. They met many volunteers on their way to Spain to fight for The Republicans in the war. They arrived in Madrid."

Raimund got up from his chair and walked to the window, he opened it and looked out, the night sounds flowed in, he stood there for several minutes and then returned .

"His brilliance at Burlesque was born in Madrid. He became well known among artists and film makers, word spread. He performed at a small theatre in the centre of Madrid. His performances came to the attention of the authorities. A large poster appeared outside the theatre mocking Franco. One evening before his performance he was told there were some important people in the audience. Those important people included Franco and his entourage and when they were in the entrance to the theatre, Dad appeared dressed as The Mad Hatter from Alice through the looking glass and flaunted in front of Franco. Photographs were taken of a furious Franco being made to look ridiculous. Here are the photographs Jack."

There was The Mad Hatter draping himself around Franco while the other cast members were dancing through Franco's party.

"The theatre was closed that night, paintings were smashed and in the confusion Dad, Mother and the cast fled. That was Dad; the pompous should be ridiculed."

Raimund showed me the route to the volcano. It was a long day, out until dark, we started before dawn, taking the same route as the day before, climbing the hill behind the house and then into wild country. There was a stout breeze which whistled through the trees until shelter in a long rivered valley where rapids sped over the boulders to end in tranquil pools and then to speed on again. We climbed out of the valley and on to the slopes of the volcano. The breeze had dropped. It took us two hours to reach the top. The view was enormous, other islands, the Pacific stretching, not even a ship. We sat by the crater, long silent, ate, walked on the top and took a different path down reaching home with dusk approaching. Tired and satisfied, a meal left for us. Raimund poured two large whiskeys and we sat staring out of the window, not speaking. "Dad loved his whiskey!" He said eventually. We ate in silence and then moved to the veranda.

"Dad and Mother escaped Spain. He felt he had let down those he had worked with, but it was either flight or the firing squad. It was 1937 and they travelled to Berlin. You would have thought that after his parents having fled Germany it would have been the last place to go to. They stayed for a year. Mother was sought after for her outrageous costumes and Dad for his extraordinary routines at the clubs and theatres. And then of course the attention from the authorities. It was brutal. He was arrested, held by the Gestapo, beaten up, warned and released! For the sake of Mother they decided to return to South America. Dad had one last performance before leaving Germany." Raimund supplied more whiskey.

"He went to Nuremburg by himself, equipped with a white rabbit costume. The evening before one of Hitler's rallies he smeared himself with engine grease, put the costume on, wrapped himself in a large coat, put the head of the white rabbit in a case and made his way to the rally. History does not tell us how he got on the rostrum, passed guards, shed the over coat, put on the head and climbed up beside Hitler, ranting, but he did. I think the guards were so surprised that they thought it was part of the rally. He was beside Hitler for a full minute prancing around him. Even the crowd yelled in approval. He removed the costume when he knew the game was up, dressed only in his underpants, his body glistening with the grease, he slipped through the crowd. The picture that you were looking at, if you study it carefully, you can see the discarded rabbit outfit."

I peered at the picture and there at the back of the rostrum was the costume, the head standing upright, looking out at the crowd with lifeless eyes.

"There is a movie picture I have been told of that wonderful moment; I've never been able to locate it. Mother had returned to Paris and talked Dad out of a meeting with Mussolini. That was a dictator too far!"

Raimund stayed at home the next day. I took a path that would lead me to a fisherman's hut. "Her name is Jana, I think you will find her an interesting person," he said as I set out. The path stayed close to the sea, and after the exertions of the previous days, it was a relief to be on the flat. I moved along rapidly, taking in my surroundings, when I saw, on the path, a frog. It was in distress, exposed to the beating sun. I squatted down to remove it from the path. I picked it up and placed it among the foliage, and as I removed my hand, its front legs folded over its head to protect itself. I had an immense feeling of belonging. The frog had been at my mercy, I could have done anything, but that act with its legs made me feel humble and recognise the fragility of the world. I watched it for minutes and saw it gaining strength. I slowly backed away and continued on my trek. That little creature has remained in my memory since.

I reached the hut in the early afternoon. There was no one there, I sat and waited. After an hour I heard somebody approaching from the forest and saw a woman and then a man. They had seen me and welcomed me. Jana and Sanda. She was an islander and he was French.

I stayed for four days. Jana said that Raimund would understand my extended time away.

The memory that stays with me was a night sailing on their outrigger to a remote island. Where they had a rough shack. We left at sunset, steering by the stars. I looked at Jana and Sanda, we were in the presence of the spirits of the night, the belonging returned and I thanked Raimund for this exceptional experience. The craft smacked through the water, the sail catching the gentle night breeze. The island appeared from the darkness; Jana slackened the sail, the boat glided through a gap in the reef, into the lagoon and on to the beach. The night sounds from the forest greeted us as we walked to the shack. Sanda soon had oil lamps glowing and a fire crackling in a shallow pit.

We talked until late, about the islands, the sea, the fish, whales, navigating by the stars, about many things, it didn't matter, it was just good to talk. We turned in for the night and I was soon asleep, woken by the sun climbing over the horizon into a clear sky.

We tramped the island, crossed to other close islands until it was time to return. I left Jana and Sanda and returned to Raimund.

24

I reached Raimund's house and knew that something was not right. There was a chair lying on its side on the veranda, a window by the front door had been broken. I knocked, no answer, calling out, no reply. Walking round the back, pot plants had been smashed, undergrowth had been flattened, a railing on the rear veranda broken. Pushing on the front door; it gave way, I went into the living room. The evidence of a struggle was everywhere. I searched the house, Raimund had gone.

My eye was caught by the small sound system that he often used to play his music on in the evenings. A light was blinking on the box and then there was a click. The Rhapsody filled the room, I stood staring out at the Pacific, my emotions torn. I must have been there for about five minutes before I could gather myself. The music stopped. I was brought alarmingly to the present by a helicopter crossing the sea in front of the house. Of course, the smashed pot plants, the flattened undergrowth. It would have been a difficult landing, but that was how Raimund had been snatched. After all these years they had got him. Had I led them to him? That question churned in my mind. Were they looking for me now?

I talked to the fishermen; they had been on the sea. I went to the town where I had landed on the island, nobody knew, except to say that he usually came into town once a week, he hadn't appeared. I was alone and isolated, and fear was eating me. I booked my passage back to Papeete on the next ship, secured Raimund's house and left.

Raimund had disappeared. I tried to find him, visiting Lucia, running short of money, Jessica was distraught at my state of mind, the children, now almost adults, were worried for me. My life had been taken over in my quest to find him.

Then the local post office telephoned one morning and

told me there was a package to collect. I wasn't expecting anything but told them I would be in the next morning. By this time my search for him had been exhausted and I was back to fishing and leading my old life on the beach. Jessica and the children had supported me throughout the search, but I had to face up to it, I wasn't going to find him. I had kept in touch with Lucia, now elderly, and with Xlia, they had realised the awful truth, Raimund was no more.

I drove to town to pick up the package. It was wrapped in bright red paper and stood out on the parcel shelf as soon as I entered the post office. I signed for it and returned to the pick-up. Inspecting the package, trying to make out where it came from, I carefully undid the paper, an inner layer which slid off, revealing a manuscript running to hundreds of pages, written in long hand. I flicked through. A loose paper fell to the floor. I picked it up. It was a letter addressed to me and as I suspected it was signed off *Raimund*.

My dear Jack.

It is now many years since I was seized from the island. I have had no contact with the world and have no idea whether you, Lucia, Xlia and my friends have been searching for me. You have in your hands the story of my life over the years. I would like you to deliver these pages to my publisher in Berlin. She knows me well and has published all my books. Contact her before you go, she will arrange money, air tickets and accommodation. Her name is Marianne. Her address is on the first page of the manuscript.

Jack, you have been a good friend, the best and I know you will remain so. Lucia, Xlia and friends have been watched for years, so I must entrust this task to you. Do you remember years ago I gave you a CD when you were leaving Rome to return to Australia? Please listen to it carefully, there is more than birdsong.

I'm sure Jessica and the children are exasperated by the

time you have spent closely entwined in my life. It will have been worth it. Send love to them from me and one day I hope to stand on that beach again and watch the waves pounding in.

Now keep the manuscript well guarded, it is the only copy. Read it and don't ask how it got to you, please get it to Berlin soon. My brother Joseph and his partner Jurgen live in Berlin, Marianne will introduce you.

Your friend, Raimund.

I drove home deep in thought. Jessica greeted me. I told her everything. We both looked at the manuscript and as usual she was supportive of what I had to do.

I spent a week reading, between the fishing and the whale watching.

My first days of captivity, I spent trying to find out where I was. I had been taken by aeroplane from Papeete for many hours. My captors hardly spoke to me during the flight, I was blindfolded except for eating and visiting the lavatory. When I did see their faces they never looked at me. The man who did speak, spoke with an American accent. The flight lasted for about eighteen hours. When we landed, there was a long wait, and after leaving the aeroplane, my blindfold removed, I was taken to a solitary building, amidst a vast expanse of snow covered country.

I read through the afternoon. The light faded. Raimund coming back into my life. The journey to Berlin. I didn't want the interruption. The business was doing well, but I needed to help him.

I was driven from the building to an enclosed area. There were huts , rows upon rows. I was placed in one and there I remained for years. I was never told why I was there, nobody spoke to me. I spoke to my gaolers, they never replied. There was a small space outside my hut where I could walk. Distant hills, nothing moved on those hills, seasons changed. There were other prisoners, we tried to communicate, voices didn't travel. I was never ill-treated, the isolation, the loneliness, that was my torture. I always knew my ideas and my deeds had terrified governments and corporations. I believed that we had been collected and among us were the agitators, philosophers, artists, writers. We were here so diversity was not able to fly. One time I was moved to another part of this prison for only a day and then returned to my hut, I saw on the gates in massive letters 'We will collect all of you.'

I read the manuscript over two weeks. How had he got the paper and pens to write? How did he get the final draft out of the prison? Maybe the people holding him wanted it that way as a warning to others. When I had finished, I phoned Marianne in Berlin and told her I was ready to deliver. She said she would arrange the flights, money, and accommodation. I looked for the CD that Raimund had given me. More than bird song, he said. I searched the shack for it, lost.

25

I arrived in Berlin. A man approached me at arrivals. "Jack, I'm Raimund's brother, Joseph."

The hut was my world. I withdrew into myself, but I had visitors. In my second summer, one evening I was aware of a low buzzing sound at the front of my hut over the door frame. I saw bees entering a hole between the frame and exterior of the building, it was a nest. If only I could get at the honey. Inspecting the inside of the frame I found a way to the honey by removing a small panel. I was careful, avoiding being stung, sliding my plastic knife through the gap and making contact with the comb. Removing the knife, it was laden with sparkling honey. I gorged on it, the sweetness was almost too much after my bland rations. I never took too much of the honey, I wanted the bees to remain and supply me with this luxury.

A brilliant butterfly used to visit in the Spring and remain until the end of the Summers. It couldn't have been the same one each year. It would alight on the white exterior of the hut and sometimes land on my shoulders or head. What was this sense that it displayed every year? I would like to think that it was the spirit of somebody I had once known. It appeared without fail and when the weather cooled, it left.

The swallows arrived in the Spring, swooping low over the compound, landing on overhead cables, twittering, returning to last year's nest, raising their young, and then off on the long migration.

But I digress. After three years, I was moved into another part of the prison, where I could mix with other prisoners. It was a shock to be with people again. There were both male and female prisoners. It was tightly regulated in the communal area. I saw faces I recognised, a Nobel laureate maybe, a writer of children's books perhaps. I tried to put names to the faces. Speaking a few words to my companions was all I was allowed, before being told to stop. I could not understand the reasons for being here, to snuff out difference was the only thing I could think of.

It sometimes seemed that I was treated differently. I was referred to as The Politician. Let me tell you about the people I met. The more I mixed, the cannier I became in communication even to the point of lip reading, our own signage with hands and feet. I became friends with an elderly lady, she must have been in her eighties. For what reason do you lock up a person of that age, did she threaten world order? She was English and had been the writer of children's books.

Her story came out over the weeks. Since the surveillance was keen in the compound ,time together was soon stopped but in our passings the stories were told. I never knew her name. She had been arrested when she was leaving New York to travel to London and had been transferred over many days to this prison. No official spoke to her, nobody answered her questions. Five years had passed since her capture. Her books and there had been many, told of strangers visiting the Earth and teaching us different ways of conducting ourselves, these strangers lived among us and took many forms. They were not violent, they didn't coerce, but out of these meetings weird and magnificent things happened.

She had travelled the world collecting the stories. The more remote the people the better. She sought out Shamans, they were some of the best observers of the world and she wove children's tales from what they told her. I told her of my experience in Cambodia, the Shaman who had helped the villagers.

I noticed that she was becoming frailer over the months and I attempted to alert those in charge of her condition. Nobody listened, nobody spoke. She died one winter's night. It was a brutally cold night and I heard a commotion in one of the huts. They must have been removing her body. I tried to look over the partitioning walls but apart from flashing torch lights, I saw nothing. In the compound days later there was a feeling of loss. I particularly felt it, and when passing one of the prisoners, he said "She knew too much." Nothing more. Had they killed her? Some of the prisoners referred to her as Elena, I grieve for her.

I wish I knew where I was, the bees continue to supply

me with honey, the butterfly visits during the long Summer days. My time mixing with others is abruptly stopped. I didn't leave the hut perimeter for weeks. Food is delivered, the deliverer never speaks, never looks at my face. He has been the same man for a long time. How long can he show not a trace of humanity? I decided that that would be my project, to try and start a dialogue with him. I was sure that overtime he would respond.

The winter nights were long and my visitors wouldn't be back until the Spring, but I had been given paper and pens and so I started this manuscript. There must have been a motive behind this one kindness but silence was the supreme sense here, nobody would tell me. While in a deep sleep one night I was woken by a magnificent operatic female voice soaring through the compounds. I lay there drowning in this exquisite sound. It was the first time, apart from mumbled conversations with other prisoners, that sound had travelled and for all to hear. I couldn't place the opera but I knew I had heard it when I was young with Mother and Dad. I wondered how long the singer could sustain this aria before she was silenced, but she finished it. What would be her punishment?

I tried to start conversations with my overseer, it was impossible. I couldn't even make eye contact with him. Then again one night the opera singer made our imaginations fly. This time a different aria but with dire results. After about two minutes, silence. I could hear raised voices, the slamming of doors, then nothing. We were all forced into the exercise area the next morning. A woman was brought through from a different part of the camp. She was a black woman in her forties, a rope was placed round her neck and she was hanged from one of the lighting gantries. I stared in horror and thrust myself forward between the guards, I was thrown to the ground and kicked.

That was the first orgy of violence I had witnessed and

also the first time apart from my capture that I had been subjected to aggression. We were returned to our huts. I felt the shock of seeing the hanging, it entered my dreams. I woke in the small hours fretting. I shouted at my guard, "Fucking talk to me!" Nothing. The opera ceased. I record all this in my manuscript. Nobody tried to stop me, nobody read what I was writing. Eventually I was allowed out to the exercise area and I made my way to where the woman was hanged. I stood looking to the sky, wondering who she was and why she had been brought to this place. I kicked a pebble over to the hanging spot, a small gesture to an unknown woman with a beautiful voice.

I had often noticed a young good looking man shuffling round the perimeter, always by himself. He never tried to lock in with the groups or to make a friend with loners. I got close to him one day and saw that he had a withered right hand. Perhaps he felt an outsider because of his deformity. He was willing to speak, his English was not good but then I realised that Spanish was his language. Our conversations were held over many months, snippet by snippet.

When the guards saw us loitering together for more than a few minutes, we were moved on. He had been transported from a village near Granada and when he arrived in the camp, they crushed his hand so he would never play the guitar again. His name was Leonardo and he came from a famous musical family who indulged their passion for Flamenco. After they had crushed his hand, they presented him with his favourite guitar by placing it in his hut. When he told me this his eyes welled. I put my hand on his shoulder. He missed everybody and didn't understand anything now.

26

Joseph drove me into the city. He had rented an apartment for my stay. It was big, grand and old, reached by either a rickety lift or a wide winding staircase. He said that a friend owned the property who was away in South America.

"We will meet with Marianne tomorrow, tonight you will come to eat with me and my partner Jurgen, but first get some rest, it is your home, I'll collect you at seven"

I collapsed on to the bed for an hour and then explored my home. I unpacked and sat on a small balcony overlooking a busy tree lined avenue. I thought back over the years and my friendship with Raimund. The places, the people I had met, the knowledge I had gained, none of it would have happened if it hadn't been for that chance meeting on my beloved beach. But the dark side was always present, and this was the reason for being here. I was excited by this latest turn in Raimund's life. But at the same time I felt fearful as to how it would end. What were Marianne and Joseph going to add to the story?

Joseph and Jurgen picked me up and we spent the evening at a restaurant.

"I run a small book publishing business in Berlin. I'm sure Raimund told you about Mother and Dad and their world of Burlesque, well I have continued with Dad's love of that type of theatre. It is well received in Berlin. When I'm not busy with the publishing, I manage a small theatre. Marianne helps me. These are difficult times for the arts, they are difficult times for anybody with new ideas and I know that is why Raimund was removed."

He paused for a few moments and then continued.

"I will spend some time reading the manuscript and then we must consider what is to be done. Raimund was much closer to our sister Lucia than I was. I was away a lot in my early twenties. I lived in Portugal for two years before moving here. In the years before he disappeared we had got together again. Now that democracy has returned to Argentina, I have pursued the people that murdered Mother and Dad, but those responsible have closed ranks and maintain a silence. They are elderly now but I will continue to pursue them. I have many friends in Argentina who tell me about what is happening. They also have friends and relatives who have been murdered. A good friend of mine who was a well-known artist here in Berlin disappeared last year, nobody has heard from him since."

"The police officer dealing with the case and who we believe was near to finding out what had happened was shot dead about five months ago, nobody has been convicted of his murder. This is what we are dealing with. Before I read the manuscript, I knew about the movement to crush dissent. Those who are not removed from society and sent to camps are dealt with in their homes.Whoever is doing this is removing or destroying their ability to create their art. What will they do to Raimund? Raimund will say what he thinks and this will be his death warrant. The role of art is to change us."

We sat in silence, I was attempting to take all this in. We left the restaurant late, Joseph dropped me off at the apartment and said he would call for me at ten. I was now wondering whether I should stay on in Berlin, forget what I had heard, forget about Raimund, return home to the beach. I had had these thoughts before, but I had become a part of Raimund's life, the dangers and the good times, I knew I couldn't do it.

I phoned Jessica, I calculated that it was night in Australia. She needed to know my plans. I woke her out of a deep sleep. "You must continue Jack, with all you have been through you must see it to the end. Joe is looking after the fishing, the restaurant is always busy, the kids are fine." I told her I would be back soon whatever happened. See it to the end. I contemplated what the end might be. I didn't think that this had an end. The artist who disappeared, the murdered policeman, it was spiralling into unknown territories.

Joseph took me to his office. I met Marianne. She was in her forties, long plaited blond hair, tall, blue searching eyes. Reading glasses rested on a long straight nose, a broad welcoming face. She was dressed like a company director. A dark suit and white blouse. She hugged me, I was taken aback but I'm sure it was because I was a friend of Raimund. She filled three glasses with red wine even though it was only eleven in the morning. "We have much to discuss over the days."

27

I met many others in the camp, and in the usual way, their stories were told. Then one night while lying on my bed, I heard a noise outside my hut. I got up and peered into the darkness. The gate to my space was ajar. Slowly stepping outside and over to the gate I pushed it open and stared down the narrow walkway between the compounds. I was aware of a figure over to my left, I was sure it was my guard. I had known him for five years. Was this his moment of humanity towards me? Aiding my escape. Over those years no conversation had ever taken place between us, but in the last months I had felt a profound change in him. After the years of avoiding eye contact, our eyes would meet and I could see a deep pain and a longing to shed the load he carried within himself.

Although it was a spring night, it was cold. I returned to the hut, gathered my few possessions and walked away. I saw a piece of paper on the ground; I picked it up and put it in a pocket. I followed the path between the huts, through another unlocked gate and into a treeless expanse of country. The moon lit my way, I didn't look back, I had no idea where I was, I was free.

I walked for hours. I had retrieved a stale piece of bread, left over from yesterday's lunch. It would have to do until I found a source of food. I walked towards the rising sun. How long would it be before my escape was discovered? What would happen to my guard? I hurried on over the unending flat land. Reaching a river, I sat and ate the bread. An aeroplane flew high overhead and my instinct was to slide down the bank and on to some shingle, knowing there was no possibility of the occupants seeing me. I rested for an hour and then continued. I felt totally lost. There were no clues as to where I was.

I followed the river downstream, looking for fish which might have given me hope of food, but it was deep and fast flowing. Hunger invaded me. The day was ending when I saw trees in the distance. It took me many minutes to reach them and when I did I threw myself on the ground, exhausted. I remembered the piece of paper. I took it from my pocket. There was writing on one side. The English was faltering, but it expressed a deep desire for freedom. "Go, take my spirit with you, away from the anger that surrounds us. You showed me another way with your graciousness. I will always remember you." And that was all.

The sun was going down, I put the note in a deep pocket, I didn't want to lose it. I stared into the distance. I was deeply moved by those few lines.

I needed food, I saw a low tree where a small bird was flying back and forth to a hole in the trunk. Necessity drove me to reach into the hole and remove two eggs which I cracked open and emptied the contents into my mouth, it wasn't much, but I hoped it would sustain me through the coming night. A hollow in the ground was my bed; I pulled leaves and dry twigs over me in an attempt to keep warm.

A breeze was rattling through the tress when I woke. The little bird was still visiting the hole in the tree. I moved from my hollow and walked to the edge of the trees. In the far distance a figure was walking across the skyline. I retreated back into the shadows. I watched. It was approaching my refuge. I saw a small man, dressed like a monk; a long sweeping garment flowed behind him, a staff in his hand and a conical hat on his head. Twenty paces behind him a dog ran hither and thither. I was immediately reminded of the shaman in Cambodia all those years ago.

Should I make my presence known? I didn't have to; he came straight to me and held out his hands in greeting. "I knew you would be here, you must be hungry. I will take you to my home where you can stay. Come." We started off over the land. How did I understand him? How did he find me? The answer to these questions would have to wait. We walked for many hours, the dog frolicking along beside us. We reached a wooded valley and then a small settlement. The few people I saw as they stared at me from the fields where they were cultivating crops were of far eastern origin as was my guide.

28

Marianne and Joseph whirled me around Berlin, where history had collided. I remembered Lucia saying this of Raimund's troubled trip to the city many years before. The evenings were dedicated to the manuscript and how we were going to find Raimund. He had escaped and was now wandering with no communication and as far as we knew and without contacts. We must alert somebody to what was happening, but who? The world of government may be complicit to these events.

His name was Belf and he told me what I had already guessed, that he was a shaman. I was in the north, no country name, no mention of cities. Their world, the plains, a mountain range and the valleys. I stayed with Belf for many months. He talked of the world inflicting hurt upon itself through constant war and conflict. The stories of the world centred around these conflicts and that we must change the story if we were to survive. I told him of my efforts and that was why I was sent to the camp. He knew of the camp but not what it did, and when I told him he was deeply troubled.

I had been at Belf's house for a month, then one night I was woken by what I thought were the wings of a bird flapping outside my window. I rose and walked to the window and looked out into the darkness. I could just make out an owl skimming across the field and over the tree tops. I was enthralled by that sight and watched the owl until it was lost from view. I was thirsty and went to the kitchen and as I passed Belf's room, I saw that his door was slightly open, moon beams falling on his bed, he wasn't in the room. I searched the house. I thought that he must have gone to tend the animals that he kept in an enclosure near the house.

I returned to my bed and slept soundly. On waking I went to make breakfast, and when passing his room I saw that it was still empty. The sun was rising and starting to flood the valley, when I saw an owl streak past the kitchen window. Minutes passed and then the front door opened and Belf came in. His face was serious, he came over to me, I saw that he had been crying. "I have been to the camp and as you said it is a place of great distress." I wanted to ask him how he could have travelled to the camp during the night as it was days away, I didn't, he patted the side of his nose with his finger. It was then that I realised. I had heard about shamans in South America taking on the form of jaguars and other forest dwellers. As he went to his room, he looked back at me and said "Leonardo asks that you find his family and tell them." I had forgotten Leonardo and felt shameful for doing so. I would find his family.

Over the days I had time to reflect on my situation. Belf would leave me and travel to the mountains, he tended a garden that he had created beside his house, he often visited the village and one day I went with him. He taught in the school and I was present when he delivered a lesson. It was a lesson I could never have imagined. It included mathematics, astronomy, philosophy. He set the children projects, they eagerly took part, the lesson ended with artwork displayed on the classroom walls.

My curiosity was aroused when leaving the school. I saw a magnificent snow leopard lying on the roof of one of the village houses, beside the leopard was a girl stroking its head. I looked at Belf, he smiled. "They are our mountain friends, they come into the village on most days and leave after the lessons are finished." We walked back to the house.

We travelled to the mountains, walking high mountain paths to monasteries situated in remote valleys, some of them perched on sheer cliffs. The monks and nuns were of Buddhist orders and the sights and sounds enveloped me and the warmth of purpose led me. Belf arranged for us to stay in the monasteries. It depended on our progress during the day which one we would stop at for the night. I inched along many of the paths since my head for heights was challenged. Belf encouraged me to overcome my fears, and as the days went by my confidence was rewarded.

We were welcomed graciously everywhere we went. Belf was known by everybody. In the lowlands people tended farms and gardens and we stayed in their houses. It appeared to be a world where conflicts were unheard of, but this feeling was discouraged when I told Belf about it. He told me that we were to attend a meeting of shamans. They were to come from all lands, it was a biannual meeting and this year it was to be held in this country. "Raimund, we have worked hard to achieve harmony, it doesn't always happen, but we talk, and if that doesn't work, we talk!"

I was present at the meeting as an observer. It was held in The High Monastery in a vast hall. The setting was one of pageantry and traditions amid the high peaks. It lasted for ten days. Men and women thronged the hall. A dazzling crowd gathered each day and listened to speeches. Departing to anterooms to continue with the business of cooperation. I wish I had been party to the meetings in those rooms. Then suddenly I was summoned by Belf to the hall. He led me out to the platform where I looked down on a packed hall. I was terrified. Belf introduced me and then asked me to tell the assembly about my experiences in the eight months of my presidency in South America.

I woke to the sound of helicopters flying overhead. I shrunk further into the hollow and attempted to pull more leaves over me. I was cold and starving. The dream still vivid in my mind. There was no Belf, no High Monastery with crowds waiting to hear me talk of my experiences, my only company, the little bird busy at its nest, the fading sound of the helicopters. My dreams brought me solace over the years at the camp, but this one had particular gravitas.

The day was warm and when silence fell I moved out of the trees on to the plains. Hunger drove me. I covered a large distance in several hours. There was no human habitation and as I despaired of finding food, a track appeared. I headed west into the setting sun.

The manuscript ended abruptly and left us with a sense of dread. We discussed, argued and debated about what to do, but not knowing what country he had been imprisoned in, and the fear of approaching anybody in authority, made us feel useless. I stayed on in Berlin for a few more days and then returned to the shack. We agreed that I would probably be the person that Raimund would contact when he emerged. It was good to be home, family, friends, the surf, sand.

Nobody had heard from Raimund for months. Marianne was often in touch with me. The hope that he would contact me never happened. It seemed that he had ceased trying to find his friends. I was always optimistic that he would just turn up one day at the shack, but as the months passed and there was still no sign, I decided to seek out Lucia.

I travelled to Melbourne and went to her house. I had not seen Lucia for a long time and was cautious about meeting her again. The house was firmly closed when I arrived. Shutters across the windows. I knocked anyway, and then went through a side gate to the garden. It was as I remembered it. The sculptures were still there. I climbed up to the veranda. Peering through a gap in a shutter, just darkness. I returned to the front and then to the road. A man approached me.

"She left six months ago, I don't know where she went, I'm looking after the house while she's gone. You're Jack aren't you? She said you might turn up." I felt uneasy with this man.

"Yes I'm Jack."

"This arrived at my home a few weeks ago. When I opened the envelope, the front page said 'For Jack' I'm not a great reader so I don't know what it's about." I felt the need to leave, I wasn't welcome, conversation was sparse. "Thanks for the information and the letter. I'll be leaving now." The man watched me out of sight.

The train back to Perth was almost empty and I spread out over the seats. The letter filled in many of the gaps in Raimund's story after escaping from the camp. It was both uplifting and disheartening but filled with hope. I decided to read it when I returned to the shack, my appetite for the contents had been sharpened by what I had read in the first pages.

I drove from Perth down the coast. Although I was excited about the letter, I still felt that unease when I met the man in Melbourne. I pulled in to the side of the road to rest and eat a sandwich that I had bought at a road stop. I had just left a small township and the countryside was scraggly bush and thorn. My attention was drawn to an old clapboard house, paint peeling, with a wide veranda at the front. An elderly man was sitting on the veranda, smoking. I watched him as I ate; he got up and moved to the side of the house where there was a variety of garden tools. He started to tend the sun scorched garden he had created. After a few minutes he looked over to me and waved. That scene in all its pure simplicity was a moment I have treasured. He approached the car, we had a short conversation, he returned to the house and then emerged with two cups of sweet strong coffee and beckoned me over. We talked and he told me of his young life in Southern Italy. I continued my journey south.

My dear Jack – Another letter! I'm sure you met Ted, my next door neighbour. Unfriendly isn't he? He is actually a wonderful neighbour. I had this letter delivered to him because I know my mail is being intercepted and I'm sure yours is as well. He always looks after my house when I'm away and he knows what is going on with Raimund. As you can gather I have been away for some time now. I am with Raimund on a Greek island where he has been for a year. He is well and the happiest I have seen him. You are always in his thoughts. He had been imprisoned in Siberia. He doesn't know who is responsible for the disappearances of the thousands of people from around the world. You probably know that most of them come from the world of arts. He suspects that powerful, influential people are those carrying out this hidden genocide. Any difference or artful talent is being silenced, they do not fit their agenda –

29

I travelled to Syros with Jessica. The kids were now at university and very capable. We flew to Athens and then by ferry to the island. It was a brilliant day when we stepped ashore on the small quayside, the light penetrated the small town and a chorus of cicadas filled the air. We were met by a young man driving a worn minibus, driven through the town, on to a rough track rising steeply through a boulder strewn hillside. After half an hour a house appeared. The driver pointed "Raimund."

Raimund came out on to the step, he was wearing a wide brimmed hat, a threadbare shirt and wide shepherd trousers. A smile covered his face, the same Raimund, a bit older. He was followed by Lucia and then Xlia. The welcoming and the joy of seeing everybody went on for minutes. We were shown to a room looking out over the hillside, trees, the distant sea.

During the days I listened to Raimund telling me of his experiences in captivity, his escape and the epic journey he undertook to reach freedom. We all walked the island together. He was known in the villages we passed through and when we returned, he would always go to a small room at the back of the house for an hour and write. He was secretive about his writing and I didn't probe. During that hour I used to walk up behind the house, sit and look out over the sea.

There were many questions I wanted to ask him. I knew

he had written about changes, but nothing explained the importance that those in power saw in his existence as a free person. I doubted that I would penetrate these secret thoughts of his, and looking at him in this house, the local clothes he wore, his simple life, it was hard to understand that he was a threat. He had told me many things but I couldn't round the circle. I shouldn't try, I liked the way it was.

We stayed a month. It was an experience I will never forget. The days filled with laughter, wallowing in the sea, eating and drinking in the local tavernas. The night before we left, I was making my way to my room, I saw Raimund's writing room was closed, light was coming from under the door, I could hear the Rhapsody softly playing. Wondering whether I should knock and spend a few minutes with him on the last evening. I didn't have to. Raimund opened the door and invited me in. He gave me a glass of wine. I looked at him in the soft light, the moonlight added to a deep feeling of well-being in the room. We talked passed midnight.

"I wish I could tell you what I know, I can't yet. I must write about it, and then and only then will I have the freedom to publish my discoveries. Marianne will be my publisher. It should be ready in a year, and you will be one of the first people to receive a copy. The last month has been a wonderful time with you and Jessica and I will miss you. I won't see you in the morning, I'm going to another island for a week and then to Spain. I met a young Spaniard, Leonardo, in the camp, I want to find his family. I wish you well Jack." Our parting was formal but the warmth between us was as always.

I was no further forward in finding out about Raimund and the information he held, and why artists, philosophers, writers were being removed from the world without anybody protesting. Those who did, and they were usually family and friends of the disappeared, were silenced. It was going to be a year before the book came out so it was time to try and unravel this puzzle that had been placed before me when I met Raimund on my beach fifteen years ago.

I started to read. I had always been a reader, but this was more than I had bargained for. I spoke to Lucia, she told me that I had a mountain of books to read if I was to understand Raimund's thoughts and actions. I was willing to try so I asked for a list to start me off. I would use my spare time reading, take the books to sea, and share my readings with Jessica and Joe.

Lucia sent me a list which included twelve books. Philosophy, the arts, biographies, autobiographies, fiction, fact. We laughed our way through a book on philosophy, not understanding a word, but making it our objective to understand. The three of us would gather in the evenings and discuss the works of Socrates. I would look at Joe and Jessica and say, "Now come on, it's written in English, we must be able to understand what he's trying to say." After several hours of discussion about a particular passage we usually came to an agreement on its meaning.

Over the months we became more and more skilled at understanding and even more at arguing about meaning. Our outlook was changing, we didn't mention it, I saw that it was most pronounced in Joe and it was good. We studied books on the history of art, we read some of the Russian classics and when making our way out to the cray pots one day, *Anna Karenina* fell into the sea. Joe dived for it, but it was wedged between the corals.

After finishing the first books Lucia supplied us with another list of six books. I think she was enjoying our enthusiasm. Eighteen months had now passed since I had seen Raimund. The pile of books grew taller and our supplier in Perth must have been wondering who I was. Our minds were full of ideas and this was when I realised the knowledge Raimund must have. The man who knew too much! Lucia told me that many years ago, one of Raimund's beloved philosophers was a woman from Ethiopia. She didn't know how he found her. Nobody had heard of her, but Raimund had visited her when she was an old lady. He would not say where she was in Ethiopia or what she told him. He wrote a book about her, there was only one copy.

Now that our curiosities were flying we begged Lucia to get the book. She said that she would try, but didn't think it would be possible, Raimund treasured it.

Lucia had heard that the hunt for Raimund was becoming intense and I was curious about this development since I thought the hunters had believed him dead after his escape from the camp. Nobody could have crossed those enormous distances in winter.

It was an altogether different side to Raimund. A wickedly satirical magazine had appeared in America for the first time and it had Raimund's name on it as the editor. The US government was beyond fury. It threatened other countries for allowing the publication, especially the Germans and most of all the city of Berlin. They were probably right. I'm sure Marianne, Joseph, and Jurgen's special ability to upset the powerful was behind the magazine. The Americans tried to stop the flow of copies spreading across the country. It was impossible, it was being given away on the street.

This news did not divert us from trying to discover who the Ethiopian philosopher was, and I pressed Lucia for the book. We felt that she had the key to Raimund's mind. I remembered Raimund saying that his book would be ready in a year, that year was well passed. Lucia said that he wouldn't be held to deadlines. We continued reading for a few more weeks. I felt saturated and chose to stop. Jessica and Joe also.

The book on the Ethiopian philosopher arrived with a letter from Lucia.

The book arrived in Melbourne a week ago. It surprised me that Raimund would allow it out of his sight. He now tells me that he travelled to Ethiopia some thirty years ago. The Ethiopian philosopher lived in the Highlands, but is now dead. She was in her nineties, a great age. You know, he attended her funeral. He said that it was an enormous gathering of tribal people from all over Ethiopia, carried out with great pomp, horseback riders, drummers, fantastic costumes. You might have noticed a painting in his house in Syros. It is of the funeral. He conveyed his memories to a painter friend of his. Keep the book carefully. The only copy! Lucia.

Her name was Hospadyr. It wasn't a long book. I read it first and then passed it on to the others. The two hundred and thirty pages were in a red leather cover. A black and white picture of Hospadyr was on the first page. She was in profile, adorned with tribal jewellery and looked very regal. I read the book over a week and when I had finished it, I left it on the veranda while I went to prepare an evening meal. It was dark and a light breeze was blowing in from the sea. I could hear the sound of the surf in the distance. The only light was in the kitchen which cast shadows across the room and out to the veranda. I was aware of a flapping sound from outside; I looked and saw a large owl standing on the table beside Raimund's book. It remained there for at least a minute looking in on me; it then bowed its body and flew off into the night. I went out and looked into the darkness.

I did not tell the others about the owl. The book was astonishing and has directed me and spoken to me in many ways – the best kind of political system run by wise old women appointed for their knowledge of the world and their judgement, uninterested in hierarchy, seeking the greatest good for the greatest number.

30

I put the book into a cupboard, I would give it to Joe next time he was this way. As I was closing the cupboard I saw the CD that Raimund had given me when I left Rome many years ago. I put it into the CD player and sat down to listen. There was birdsong for the first minutes and as it faded away a crackling female voice could be heard. She spoke very hesitant English, it was hard to understand but certain words were clear enough. The name 'Ethiopia' was mentioned on several occasions, it then fell into place. Raimund must have copied the original recording, a talk given by Hospadyr. It was going to need a great deal of concentration to listen to. I had to find the time, I would wait until Jessica and Joe had finished the book, and we would listen together.

We listened to the CD on a stormy night huddled in the shack. Hospadyr's voice and the wind outside made for an eerie atmosphere inside; we gazed into a distance that was beyond the walls. The sound faded away and then returned. She spoke of her life in Ethiopia, her love for the country, the ways, the differences, "I was raised in a village far from the capital. My father was a shopkeeper and I was one of six children, the only girl. My mother was a midwife; she travelled long distances to carry out her duties. Father saved money to send me to university; this was unusual at the time because I was the youngest and a girl. I was always grateful to him for having done this." There was a long silence in the recording, only the sound of the wind smacking around the shack. – "studying was the gate to my life, my brothers were very protective of me, three of them lived in the capital, two became doctors, one was a priest, and the other two stayed in the village, a shopkeeper and a farmer – " silence again. I walked to a window and looked out to the sea. The CD was muffled, impossible to hear. " – left the city and lived in the highlands – I had studied philosophy – lived with rural people – started a school – adults came to listen." Then clarity.

"I sit before the fire that blazes in the African night. There is a traveller out in the dark, he must be lost. His flickering shadow in the flames walking over the land. The night creatures watch him. There are others he is with a woman and children silhouetted against the night sky, they tramp their way. Often seeing those on the move with their possessions, fleeing injustice, I have become the storyteller – I am a witness. It is the story of Africa and that story must be told. I have visited the villages, towns and cities and speak for those without a voice. It has brought me into contact with differences and how they bind us.

"The traveller and his family in the dark carry with them different ways. That is their strength and they have a story. It is unfolding around us. Be aware and listen. Meeting other tribes, I have urged understanding. Many have heeded but there are those who wish to wreck dialogue that brings people together.

"Learning from the wilderness has been my most fulfilling experience, moving with nomads across the mountains, observing animals, birds, insects. They all have their part to play. Care must be taken, it is a fragile land. Strangers come to exploit, not to participate in the ways. Beware of traditions that subjugate and belittle, they are cruel, rid yourself of these, challenge those who want to keep them. Remember your home; the man, the woman and children have been driven from the things they know and cherish, however humble.

"The dawn is appearing in the east, the family have gone, the fire is dying, I go to my hut, pulling my cloth tightly round me, it is cold. I must prepare a meal. It is simple, the

coffee, life giving at the start of a day. The village is waking, people are greeting each other. I walk to the edge of the plateau, passing through a grove of trees where birds are busy, then looking over the country, an enormous distance. Movement nearby is everywhere, my gaze follows the land to the horizon and what I see is good, it is home."

Lucia told me of Raimund's life on Syros when we had left. "He always felt shame for not having tried to find Leonardo's family in Spain, he also spoke of a black lady who was an opera singer. He told me that he had witnessed her death in the camp. When you left and after he had finished some of his writing, he set off for Spain, to Granada. He spent days in Flamenco schools asking around but got nowhere in his search for information about Leonardo. He felt that they were protecting him and eventually went to a village in the mountains above Granada and there he met a travelling gypsy band, they knew exactly where to find his family. He was taken to a village by one of the elders and shown the family house.

"He was welcomed by a very noble woman in her sixties. Raimund didn't quite know how to start the conversation, he fumbled through an introduction and then said he had known Leonardo. The woman called to the back of the house, she was joined by a man her age, and five young people in their twenties, three women and two men. The woman invited Raimund in. He stood in a high ceilinged room, guitars dotted the walls and pictures of flamenco dancers cascading through their steps. His eye was caught by a painting at the end of the room. It was of the family with Leonardo staring out. He walked over to the painting and pointed to him, then looked back to the woman, tears were falling down her face."

Lucia's voice faded as if she felt the sadness of this woman.

"Raimund spent the next days at the house. He told

them about the camp and meeting Leonardo there, avoiding any mention of his hand. A strong bond grew between him and the family. They were all musicians and were famous throughout Spain and one evening they played and danced in the village square.

"He learnt that Leonardo had been snatched driving back to the village. The police investigation was quickly brought to an end and the lead detective who insisted that it continue was moved to Northern Spain and later found murdered. Raimund promised the family that he would find the people behind the disappearance and try to bring Leonardo home.

"During his stay in Spain he immersed himself in the culture and the music and after staying with the family he rented a flat in Granada and made quiet enquiries about Leonardo. It wasn't long before he met a friend of Leonardo. Her name was Celine, and she told Raimund of the extraordinary life he led. His music was of such quality that he had an enormous following in Spain. He was the eldest child in his family and he was an inspiration to many young flamenco artists. He lifted people's spirits. His grandfather was also a well known player, and was executed in the Spanish civil war. He was executed because of his love of the music.

"Raimund and Celine spent a lot of time searching archives, looking at photographs, asking friends about Leonardo, to find out why he was taken. Celine was a woman in her thirties and she had a little boy of fifteen months. Raimund would often stay with Celine and her husband Garcia during evenings. Her husband was a writer who had originally come from Portugal.

"One evening when the little boy Bondo was waiting for his bath, Celine put him in his cot and Raimund watched him romp. He was a ball of energy, snuggling his soft toys, he sped from one end of the cot to the other, an enormous grin on his face, almost somersaulting. It lasted a few minutes until the bath was ready and his mother lifted him out of the cot. It played on Raimund's mind this abandonment in the safety of the cot, the love showered on him by his parents. This love, the security of home seemed to peak at this time of day. Raimund saw the evening romp on several occasions and from this he felt memory was being formed in his young mind."

What Lucia was telling me was so profound, that I found it difficult to absorb the content without asking her to repeat much of it. I wanted to be a witness to Raimund's life at that time.

31

"Leonardo used to tramp the forests around his home, many of the trees were Spanish Cypress and from these trees the instrument makers found the wood for the flamenco guitars. He treated the trees as friends and spent many hours among them. He was a guest within this hushed assembly. The earth of Spain drew him to its heart, and he would often be seen before performances stroking and smelling the wood of his favourite guitars. These memories were buried deep within him and they carried a very special sense that intrigued and frightened people, and this was why he was taken Celine believes.

"The evening he was abducted he had played before a crowd of hundreds, it was one of his most magnificent performances. In the crowd was a group of men wearing identical black clothes. They didn't move with the music, they never clapped, they stared with blank eyes, and when the concert was over they moved towards the stage, and into the performer's area. Their presence had been noticed by many people. Leonardo was not seen again."

I heard from Raimund very rarely over the months and if I wanted to know I would telephone Lucia who was now back in Melbourne. She told me that he was continuing the search for Leonardo and trying to find out the reasons behind the abductions, his own included. I was awoken by the sound of steps on the veranda. Jessica was out at the restaurant and I was having a lie in after a long day on the sea which stretched to midnight. There was a knock on the door and I wearily made my way through the living room. I made out a figure through the gauze screen. It was Raimund.

I opened the screen and we stood looking at each other and then embraced. "Jack I should have warned you but I needed to cross the world in silence. I am still being hunted. It appears to have been unforgivable to have escaped, can you believe that? Unforgiveable, what a strange way to describe my flight from captivity and certain death."

Raimund stayed with us for weeks. Jessica welcomed him back to the beach and said that he must stay at the shack. He was very hesitant about our hospitality since he felt he was putting us at risk, which he was, but we had been at risk for years by just knowing Raimund, and anyway I had been part of this story for so long and I wanted to know the end.

Leonardo had been found and that was the reason Raimund was back in Australia. The second evening he was with us we settled in the living room over several bottles of wine and he told us about Leonardo.

"Many good people across the world were demanding reasons for the disappearances and governments were caving in to repeated protests. He was found in Granada. An early morning walker found him slumped over the fountain in the main square. He was recognised by a doctor in the hospital. Nobody knows how he was brought back and he was unable to tell anybody. He has been back in Spain for many months now. Doctors have been trying to reconstruct his hand."

"After he was found, attention was on me. Marianne contacted me from Berlin and told me to leave Syros. My pursuers knew I was in Greece and that is the reason I'm here. Lucia had left some weeks before and Xlia returned to Colombia. After I leave you I'm going to find a shack somewhere on a coast!"

I always knew that Raimund loved the shack. One day I left Raimund writing to go fishing and on my return in the evening I noticed the shack in darkness. When I went in it was obvious that Raimund had left. A note was on the table, "Jack, thank you again. Do not try to find me, I will contact you. I need to understand what is going on in the world. There are sinister people at work and I want to gather strength to oppose them, not only me but my friends, you included. I was watching two surfers today from the beach, my mind went back to our first encounter. Memory plays strange tricks, the surfers seemed to follow the same route that you followed, even passing me at the exact same spot. It made me feel very close to you and Jessica. Raimund."

So where did Raimund go? When he arrived, he had no car, and few possessions. I talked to a neighbour who told me that he had seen a lone figure walking up the road and into the dunes several hours before I returned. It must have been Raimund. I had no need to worry, Raimund had all the skills for survival.

I had a dream one night. Raimund was beckoning me down a track, through forested hillsides and then on to a beach. He stood on the beach and pointed towards a house. It must have been his shack. It reminded me of all the places where he had lived and I wondered whether he had at last found a place to settle. A place he could now feel safe in but still be in contact with the world. He never used modern communications, he always called them 'brain fryers'. He only wrote letters.

Several weeks later a letter arrived from Raimund. I opened it and took out a photograph. It was a picture of a house on a beach. I turned the photograph over and written on the back was, 'on the coast'. There was no explanation, no letter. I would have to wait. Lucia as always told me what he was doing, but not where he was. She came out west and stayed for a week.

Raimund had found his shack. He could do the things he wanted. He had set up a small printing press, a piece of technology that dated back years, he loved smelling the ink and the paper. The printing press could be heard late at night. The results taken to the nearest town and dispatched. He created a garden from the forest. He talked of a ring of fire visible from his house. He went to sea with the locals. It sounded to Lucia like his days in the Pacific, but she said there was a profound difference, his heart seemed to be at rest, his continual search for meaning had reached a destination. "I want to visit him Lucia." There was a long pause. "Go to him Jack and tell me what you find when you return."

32

I went north and crossed The Coral Sea to Espiritu Santo. There was urgency in my travelling to the island and when I stepped ashore from the small freighter I was greeted by a group of islanders. I stayed the night in the port and the next morning I was taken by car to the edge of the forest where a path led to the interior, and then to the other side of the island. My guide Tanna told me that it would take a day to reach Raimund and that I should rest in a cabin which was on the path. I would be met by a lady who watched over the sacred places on that part of the island, her name was Silentus. I was supplied with food and water and set off on the track. "Don't deviate, just keep on the main track."

I climbed through lush vegetation and as I ascended distant views of the sea, valleys, waterfalls could be seen. I had been walking for several hours when I reached a rocky outcrop where I could see my path ahead and in the distance, the cabin. The rain started to cascade down, and looking up I saw the clouds swirling and crashing into each other in preparation for the storm to come. I had to press on, thunder was approaching and lightening crowded the sky. The rain was the beginning, mighty thunderclaps echoed through the valley. I never liked being out in storms and this one was savage. I took refuge in an opening of a rock wall, I squeezed in and saw out the storm. It eventually faded into the distance. I felt privileged to have witnessed such a wild performance.

The light was fading and I had no idea how far the cabin was, I had to reach it before nightfall. I was frightened by the forest pressing in on me as the darkness fell, the dripping trees, the night sounds and my footsteps which seemed to be an intrusion in this wilderness. I then heard a voice calling, "Jack, Jack." I looked up the track and saw Silentus waving me on. I felt relief at the sound of her voice and seeing her on the path. She led me to the cabin which was set above the track, beside a small lake. She didn't speak English but we managed to communicate. I was shown to my room for the night. Before leaving in the morning she cooked me a meal and packed me some food for the journey.

The morning was still and the sun was climbing over the treetops when I started off. I wanted to reach Raimund by mid-afternoon to avoid the storms that might gather after the heat of the day. I stopped where the track fell away, seeing the sea in the distance and what I thought was a house. I started down and was eventually walking on sand. I could hear the sound of the sea, and on getting nearer another sound mixed with the waves. It was a piano. I stopped and listened. It was the Rhapsody. A smile spread across my face. I walked in the direction of the music and rounding a rock, I saw a figure on a low platform playing a grand piano. I stood, not wanting to disturb. It was Raimund. He looked towards me but continued. The music swept the beach and I saw birds, thousands, standing on the shoreline and in the shallows. Evening was approaching and an enormous shadow of player and piano spread across the sand.

I had told Lucia that I would return with images of Raimund's life. I saw a man who was at ease with himself. I wondered about his imprisonment, the things he had seen and how he had dealt with them. He led me through a story of resistance that he had mounted with the help of friends. During his years of being hunted, he had distributed his books on science, philosophy, history, politics, art, an enormous output written over many years. Some of the books had become bestsellers and many challenged the readers. The satire infuriated leaders and the comedy flattened some.

He had a deep understanding of what people yearned for, respect, truth, grace, kindness, good governance as part of a civil society. Societies free of barriers. He quoted men and women from history who had attempted all these, some had succeeded, the ideas were now part of our thinking, they could not be stopped. His belief in progress and tranquil rationalism, instead of fear and paranoia. Reason, science, education, knowledge and history should direct us.

I was becoming lost among the ideas that Raimund expounded, but it didn't matter, it was opening up a world unknown to me. He spoke of the prison. It had been exposed and leaders, who allowed their citizens to be taken, were to be put on trial. The story of Leonardo was known after Raimund had written about him, this had caused alarm among his captors and that was when he was delivered back to Spain.

The pretence of not knowing about the disappearances had shamed governments and the tide of accusations overwhelmed them. Raimund told me he wanted to find out who the black singer was, her hanging haunted him. He must do this from the shadows.

While I was with Raimund, I saw the printing press working, powered by a generator, producing the satire that he baited governments with and behind his house, in the garden there was a small brick building. One evening he led me and some of the locals to the building. Inside there was a cinema. The locals had obviously been before as they hurried to their usual places. The old projector whirred as the spools turned. We were watching a French film made many years ago. It portrayed life in Paris in the music halls, opera houses, jazz clubs, the music spilled out into the tropical night. After we had been watching for about half an hour, the scene was one of an opera house and a black female singer approached the front of the stage, her voice soared. Suddenly Raimund froze the image and walked up to the screen. He stared at the singer, it seemed for minutes. He turned and looked at me. "That's her!"

"That's who Raimund?"

"She is the lady who was executed in the camp when I was there."

Of course, I should have known. He allowed the film to finish and after the audience had left, he looked at the case in which the film had been delivered. There were two labels, one new typed label and the other old and faded, but still legible. On it was an address in Paris.

"Jack I want you to go there and find out who made this

film and also try to find out who the lady was."

I looked at Raimund in disbelief. I was on a Pacific island, no contact with the outside world, no money and Raimund wanted me to go to Paris to find out who made a film which was about forty years old, and who one of the stars was.

"Marianne will supply you with everything you need, money, hotel, travel documents, flights. I need to know, I can trust you Jack."

" Raimund I need to go home first, see the family and start the journey from there. I will do it for you but we need to discuss and plan this. I don't know what I'm taking on and I don't think you do either."

33

I arrived in Paris on a Spring evening in April, spent two days exploring the city again and then went to the address. My French was terrible; I hoped that those at the address spoke English. The house was set among apartment buildings near La Place St Michele, the area I had visited when I had met Marcel on my first trip to Paris. Although it was a sunny day, the house was grey, creating its own dullness. The paint was peeling on the door, I looked at the ground floor windows and then at the upper floor windows, heavy curtains were drawn across. There was no bell, just a heavy ornate knocker. I knocked and waited, after a minute, knocked again. I heard activity behind the door. The door opened and an elderly lady stared out, and then at me, her eyes adjusting to the bright day.

"I knew you would come, you want to see the archives, don't you? Come in." Her English was perfect.

I was startled by this welcome. I followed her into the

hall, and saw a man approaching, his hand held out. We shook hands. They were both old, but moved quickly despite their age. I followed them into the sitting room. The heavy drapes that I had seen from outside where they had looked dull and tattered, sparkled with colour. The room was brightly painted and comfortable, chairs filled the space in front of the fireplace. The man ushered me over to one of the chairs and we both sat down. The woman had gone to another room and then appeared with three glasses of wine. She was the first to speak. "My name is Eva, my husband is Hugo, you know we have been expecting somebody to call. We know about Raimund and you must be his friend Jack." I nodded," Well Jack you are welcome in our house. You must have wondered when you saw the house from the outside what you had come to. We keep it like that, it doesn't attract attention. We know about Raimund, you and the others because of Marcel, you met him last time you were in Paris."

We talked, Eva left the room, she returned later with a tray laden with food and carried it through to the dining room. During the meal Hugo told me he had been a film maker, later he would show me his work. Our conversation touched on many subjects. After we had finished eating, Eva started to talk of the disappearances, and then she mentioned the black lady. "We knew her, Hugo filmed her in the Paris opera house many years ago. He was making a film about Parisian music in the nineteen seventies, but we've lost the film of her. We think Marcel must have borrowed it. He often comes here and asks to look at our collection. We are a bit careless about keeping track of the archive."

"Eva the film is on a South Pacific island." I said.

"Goodness, however did it get there?"

We didn't mention the film again during the lunch and after finishing Hugo showed me to a room at the back of the house. It was packed with films in metal containers.

"These are all the films I have made in my lifetime Jack. I still try and get out and film. They are all documentaries. I'm eighty nine now so you know all the technology has totally changed, but I'm still using my old cameras. I don't go far from home, there is plenty of material in the streets to document. Take your time, have a look . I have to go out for an hour to see a friend, Eva will be here."

I was left in this trove of history captured on film. I looked along the titles stopping at one container that stood out in my memory. *Hitler and the white rabbit.* I removed it from the shelf and turned it over in my hands. The tape securing the container had probably not been touched since the day it had been sealed. I put it on a table and continued looking along the rows. *Hazard, Argentina.* I took it from the shelf. It was dated 1962 and the label described the film as the life of an indigenous shaman of Argentina. I felt a surge of excitement. I continued looking. They were from all over the world, a lifetime of endeavour. I thought of Raimund and how he would have loved to have been here. Had he finished that book yet?

There was a pile of vinyl records stacked in a corner. I picked up the top record and read the sleeve, The Rhapsody. Seeing an old record player in a corner of the room, I put the record on, sat in a chair, hands behind my head and listened intently while staring out at this strange room. The door opened and Hugo came in, he sat down. We didn't say anything, we just listened. When the music finished, I looked over at Hugo. He caught my gaze and smile "I've found two films I would like to see Hugo." handing him the containers. He stared for some time at *Hitler and the white rabbit.*

"My friend and assistant Antoine filmed that in Nuremberg in 1936. He got the film out of Germany and back to Paris. It is one of the most valuable films in my collection. Antoine was killed in the war, he was in the resistance. He was a wonderful friend to me. After we have eaten this evening I will show it to you. The other film you have chosen is about the life of Old Hazard. He was an extraordinary character who lived in Argentina and was one of the last shamans. People said he possessed magical powers for healing. I spent many months in Argentina in the 1960s with Old Hazard, recording his life."

"Hugo I need to know about the black opera singer. Eva said you know about Raimund, well Raimund witnessed her execution when they were both in the same prison."

"We will talk about her after we have seen the two films you have chosen. "

34

After eating, we returned to the archive where he set up a projector and pulled down a screen from one of the walls. I remembered those projectors from my childhood and when Hugo started it, it took me back to the village hall where on Saturday evenings we would gather to watch the latest films . If the film was not suitable for children, we would play in the creeks and dunes until it was over. I especially remember the motes of dust caught in the projector's beam.

An enormous crowd covered the screen and then parted as marching soldiers made their way to a raised area where the dignitaries were sitting . The camera panned over the crowd and then towards those seated. There seemed to be an air of anticipation as they waited and then Hitler strutted on to the stage. The seated stood and raised their arms in the Nazi salute. He made his way to a microphone and started to speak and quite suddenly a figure appeared on the stage. The White Rabbit. The creature darted around

Hitler and as Raimund had told me years before, when the camera panned to the crowds, there was a sense of carnival, as they laughed and yelled with joy at this spectacle. The camera returned to Hitler who was now standing looking for support from his seated uniformed staff. It was at this point that the rabbit discarded its head and rushed into the crowd, peeling off the rest of the costume, until an almost naked figure disappeared from view. The last frames showed an enraged Hitler surrounded by his officers.

Hugo looked for my reaction when he had turned off the projector. I was at first astounded, and then I laughed and laughed. I said to Hugo, "Do you know who the White Rabbit was?"

"Of course, it was Raimund's father Otto. I met him when he came to Europe and was acting in Burlesque. We spent a lot of time together in Paris. I have film of him during that time and that was when he told me about Old Hazard. We will watch that film tomorrow."

I returned to my hotel. If only I could contact Raimund and tell him about Hugo and the film archive.

I arrived at Hugo and Eva's mid-morning and was welcomed with coffee and newly baked bread. What did Raimund say about those smells, coffee and baking bread? The best smells in the world, they were that morning.

"The film is over two hours Jack; it is a fascinating look at the life of somebody who was the last of his kind and his wife who is often overlooked in the telling. But first I must show you a short film featuring Old Hazard filmed by Antoine during the Spanish Civil War in which he fought against Franco, just at the end there is a bit about his participation with the partisans in Italy." Hugo saw the surprise on my face.

"Jack when I was filming and mixing with many people, I was always perplexed as to how they fitted so much into their lives, but they did. They moved in the world because they were passionate about causes and they wanted to be part of that cause and support it. Old Hazard was one of those people. Most of his people had succumbed to disease and alcoholism and many had committed suicide. He was anything but a soldier but he felt strongly about the oppressed and wished to help. You must remember these were the 1930s and 1940s and his country was run by dictators."

"What happened to Old Hazard?" I said.

"He was shot by the regime in 1974. He had become an irritant to them, although he was living a very humble life at the time. Let's have a look at a young Old Hazard!"

Hugo turned on the projector. I was watching grainy, black and white, silent scenes of conflict when the camera settled on a young man hunkered down behind a barricade. He smiled at the camera, and it followed him as he looked over the barricade. "That's Old Hazard. "Hugo said. He was a small chunky man, laden down with equipment. He then ducked down and moved closer to the other fighters. The film followed the actions of others and then faded. It had only lasted about five minutes and then it cut to a group of men and women posing in front of a railway station. Hugo told me it was somewhere in Northern Italy. The camera went slowly along the faces and then stopped at Old Hazard, easily recognisable from his time in Spain. He was smiling and playing up to the camera.

"Antoine didn't know Old Hazard then and was surprised when the same man appeared in Spain and Italy and that was when he started to take an interest in him and which finally led Antoine to South America."

We settled to watch the film. Hugo produced two bottles of wine and Eva placed a tray of food in front of us. "You will need it!" She said as she left the room.

My perception of Old Hazard's life as a young boy entered my senses. The same feeling that I had had on the

Australian coast. He was with his mother and father in the countryside. They were living as the indigenous people of Argentina would have lived on the vast grasslands. There was a group of huts, people talking and preparing food. His mother was holding his hand and laughing with the women. A man approached and showed them an animal that he had trapped.

Old Hazard walked the grasslands with other boys. They found birds' nests in the sparse trees, they burrowed for roots and picked the edible plants. Rivers flowed through the grasslands which teemed with fish. He spent days by himself walking the rivers, catching fish with a primitive net. And as his life progressed, his relationship with the natural world was one of partnership, he handled venomous snakes and spiders, he slept out, fashioning simple shelters from materials he scavenged.

I saw his marriage to a girl in the tribe. He still followed his lifestyle, his wife accompanying him on his expeditions, and then the cattle ranchers moved on to the tribal lands. The village was burnt and the people fled to the pampas. I saw a European man with the tribe. It was Raimund, a young man. The villagers were in the process of building shelters near a wide river, but soon the ranchers destroyed those as well. The tribe moved on, they were never allowed to settle. A house appeared, it stood alone, the tribe went to the house and a woman welcomed them and she asked them to stay.

I was brought to the present by Hugo's voice. I told him how I had seen Old Hazard as a young boy and man, he listened and then said, "That's how it was."

He started the film, Old Hazard was portrayed over several years. I saw Raimund and Lucia in parts of the film, and then towards the end, Raimund's mother and father. Old Hazard was running his shop, he went to the country and it was here that the shaman traditions were practised and his powers of healing were sought. Then a mystery was solved for me, The Rhapsody. In his life the music had played an important part. He carried an ancient wind up gramophone with him loaded on a horse and during his healing sessions the music was played. The news of this therapy spread rapidly and the healing qualities were copied by many and thus The Rhapsody became a shaman tradition.

"Music holds this therapy for many people, the powerful despise this." Hugo said after the film had finished. "Art provides sustenance and comfort, that is why so many artists have disappeared."

"Serena, the opera singer was an American. She started singing in New Orleans, her first love was jazz. She was well known in that world and over the years she developed a passion for opera. That disappointed many of her fans, but she soon had an enormous following. It was the 1960s and 1970s in America and the fact that a black woman was singing opera was not accepted by many. She continued and moved to Paris. Jack, her voice was quite marvellous. Her name was Serena Staffords, she didn't return to America, she travelled in Europe singing in the great opera houses. It was at this time that she disappeared. She was adored even by those who were not drawn to opera. I met her in the 1970s in Paris."

We ate and drank some of the delicious food Eva had left us. Hugo continued. "When she wasn't at the opera house, you could see her at the jazz clubs. I remember her giving a performance in a small theatre in a poor Paris suburb. Crowds thronged the street. They had placed speakers in the streets around the theatre, that's how much she was loved. And then the music stopped. Nothing was said in the news. There were gatherings demanding to know what had happened to her. The police said nothing, but there was one police inspector who gathered a group of officers together and they started to investigate. They were dismissed from the force."

"A pattern was emerging. I had known other artists and writers during my filming, many of them vanished. I got to know Raimund in South America. He was young then and I also met Lucia. Raimund had grand ideas, it didn't surprise me that he became a president if only for eight months. I wish I had filmed some of that time, he upset many people, his intentions were good if naïve. I kept up with him through the years. We met on many occasions here in Paris, and on the last trip he spoke of you and your beach. If I were younger I would visit the southern continent. I love the wild places and I made a film in Africa years ago in the Kalahari. It was like opening a book, I spent nine months there and immersed myself in that extraordinary place, the people, the countryside, but that is another story."

"Raimund wants to know about Serena, I have no other information on her, who her family was, where she lived, nothing. What I do have is the name of the police inspector who attempted to find her. I got to know him well. His name is Max Gerard, he now lives in Briancon in the French Alps, a charming man." Hugo handed me a piece of paper with his address on it.

My time with Eva and Hugo came to an end, there was no more they could tell me. Hugo's story was more than I had hoped for, and had urged me to find an answer to the relationship I had with Raimund.

35

From Paris I took a train to Berlin and went to Marianne's office. When I arrived it was closed, even though it was mid-morning. I looked through the darkened glass of the door but could only see the outlines of the furniture. Other offices in the building were at work. I went to the next office and was told that they hadn't seen Marianne for several days. "Was this unusual?"

"Yes it was, she always tells us if she won't be in."

I tried phoning. No answer. I had an address so I went by subway and then walked. The apartment was in an old Berlin building and on approaching I saw police cars parked outside. I walked to a children's play area that was opposite the front door of the block and watched. Four men dressed in dark clothing carrying a coffin left the building, put the coffin in a van and drove away. I slowly walked to the door, looked at the police officer who was on guard, looked inside the hall and left. I needed to get away, as far as possible.

I contacted Jurgen and Joseph. "Yes we know, the police have been to see us this morning. She was murdered Jack. You must come to us while you are here." Joseph gave me directions to their apartment, I hurried through the crowds, not knowing what they could do for me, I just wanted contact with people I knew.

"Marianne had been publishing the satirical magazines and many of them had riled governments. She was threatened and told to stop. She didn't and this is the consequence. I would go back to your beach." Joseph sounded panicky and frightened. I told him about Eva and Hugo in Paris, and the films that I had seen and then said "Joseph, I have one last place to visit before returning. Hugo gave me an address of an ex police officer who had attempted to investigate the disappearance of Serena. I want to see him and ask him about her."

"Then you must return to Australia for your safety." Joseph said, "You know too much, you would be a great catch for the dispatchers."

I left Joseph and Jurgen and travelled to the French Alps. My thoughts of Marianne, her murder, was more than I could manage, I had to see Max Gerard. I went by train from

Berlin, back to Paris and then to Briancon. The Alps towered, snow on the high peaks, the air pure. I climbed down from the train and found a small hotel near the station. I showed the lady at reception Max's address and she pointed to a decrepit chalet across the street. "That's where Max lives, he is well known in the town, outspoken, awkward, but a good local politician, he used to be a policeman. He came too close to exposing the useless, he was told to leave and has made his home here. He's always out in the mountains and that's where he probably is now."

I went to the chalet later in the day, it was starting to get dark. I could see a light in a back room. I rang the bell, waited and hoped he spoke English. Max came to the door, he spoke perfect English. Hesitantly I said "I'm here about Serena Staffords, I was told by Eva and Hugo in Paris that you know about her." At this a broad smile.

"Come in, come in." I was shown into a sitting room which was tumbling with books. A woman came from another room and introduced herself. "I'm Max's wife, Simone, please sit down."

I stayed a night in the hotel, and the next day Max transported my belongings to the chalet. I was to stay for as long as I wished. My bedroom looked out over a flower filled valley to the mountains beyond.

"I have a rucksack for you, we will walk and maybe stay in mountain refuges on some nights." My stay with Max and Simone lasted two weeks. We were out every day. Max knew the mountains intimately. We trod paths that were only known to him and a few other guides. He talked and talked. Simone would raise her eyebrows and smile. I felt secure here, Max knew the dangers, he challenged them. He told me about Serena Staffords, but first he told me about his passion for Iberian literature. I was lost, but to listen to somebody with such knowledge on a subject was cathartic. He shone a light into the darkest places.

"Serena Staffords, she came from Ghana and went with her parents to America. Her father was a doctor and her mother was a teacher. They had a lot of hope and faith in America to the extent that rather than go and live in a city they went to a small community in Mississippi. This was the 1950s and although her parents were highly qualified they suffered from quite awful discrimination. They were driven out of town and ended up in New Orleans. Life was better and that is where Serena started to sing. She was sixteen. She was soon noticed by the club owners and work was easy to get, and at the same time the record companies recognised her talent and tried to sign her up. Serena wasn't interested, she just loved to sing. The record companies became obstructive and spread gossip about her, none of which was true. If they couldn't earn money from her nobody else would."

"She trained as an opera singer, she continued to sing in the jazz clubs. The critics hated her in America and so did much of the public. They couldn't swallow the fact that a black person produced such an exquisite voice."

"She moved to France, they loved her. Memories were long in America and they resented her moving and her following in Europe. She was marked for disappearing. The disappeared, I worked, when I was in the police on several other cases where musicians had disappeared, so I was experienced with this crime. I had heard that it was happening in other countries. I could never quite understand the reasons behind artists being removed. I had my own theories which I will tell you about later. I saw her performing, magnifique! I don't know what has happened to her."

"I do Max." I said. I then told Max about Raimund, the camp, the execution of Serena. He got up from his chair and walked to the window. He stared out for minutes. The light was fading over the valley, a breeze ruffled the meadow flowers. Simone came into the room.

"Jack I know you must go back to Australia. I would like you to contact your friend Raimund, I want to meet him. The world of art crosses barriers and brings new ideas. The powerful want to stamp on the new. Raimund, you tell me was a politician, well his progressive ideas were probably despised. And that's why he was taken. We live in worrying times. Serena had a brother and sister, I am still in touch with them so I will have to tell them. You must stay in touch when you leave Jack. I will visit you, Simone has always wanted to visit Australia. I had a son once, he left home when he was eighteen, we have never heard from him, so look out for him as you travel across the world. His name is William."

I returned to Australia. I had been away long enough and I was yearning for the family, the beach, the shack and the surf. I would leave contacting Raimund until I had thought everything through that I had seen and had been told. Was listening also dangerous now? I did write a short letter to Raimund and told him about Serena and that I would be contacting him. It was good to be still, to be in my own bed, to be surrounded by the familiar.

36

"Come over here Raimund." I shouted. He walked over to where I was standing, looking out to sea, watching a dense flight of birds crossing the sky in front of us. "They are navigating their well-known pathways," Raimund said, "They are truly nomadic, untouched. It is two years since I have seen you Jack. I have travelled to find people who are separate from the world as we know it. I have left the book I was writing on the island, and with instructions that it does not leave this place. It was good to listen to you telling me about Hugo and Max, and at the same time uplifting that memories are being kept alive, memories of Serena. How awful that somebody of such talent is eliminated from the world. She has a place that is forever hers."

" William, Max's son, I came across a young man navigating a craft among the reefs, he was a European. He stayed a night at my place and was gone in the morning. Conversation was not easy with him, but he said he wanted to return to France to find his parents, he spoke of the wild places he had visited. He reminded me of myself as a young man, but a home beckoned. If you are ever in touch with Max again, tell me if it was their son and that he has returned. I need to know, and his name, it was William. He told me that he wanted to listen, to be generous, and to understand the other."

I had been with Raimund for a week and that same person was weaving his story, but there was an edge I had not seen before in Raimund. He seemed impatient. Impatient with the world. He was deeply sad about Marianne but was more insistent than ever that pressure be kept on governments to change, to learn from the past, he didn't see it happening. They continued with their destructive habits. I felt that he had reached a time in his life where he as an individual had tried and his efforts had been obstructed. He must be seventy now, in all the years I had known him, I had never asked his age, he was a person where the years had no meaning.

I went home, I had time to ponder, I thought about our first meeting again, the travels, the people I had met. None of this would have happened if I hadn't invited him back to the shack that day on the beach. I was glad for it all, even the dangers. It had opened my horizons, my mind to possibilities. What of the stories of all those people? Hugo had died, and several months before his death, a letter arrived at the shack, it was from Eva. She told me of his decline. When his will was read, I was mentioned and one of his films had been left to me. I was flattered by this. She said that she would dispatch it as soon as possible and when Jessica and I were cosied into the shack on a cool blustery day, there was a knock on the door, Jim the postman delivered a parcel from France.

I rolled it around in my hands, excited by the feel of the paper, the stamps, the postmark. I opened it. I would need a projector, I didn't know anybody with one. There was a short letter from Hugo.

Dear Jack, something for you to think about and to try to understand. I didn't make the film, it was sent to me by Max Gerard, remember the policeman from Briancon. When you have seen it please tell Raimund. My health is not good now and my days are closing. There was something about you that stirred confidence. Keep going Jack. Hugo.

I searched the coast for somebody with a projector, but nothing. On the verge of giving up I asked Jim the postman and he told me about Bill Treavis. He thought he had one, but didn't have a telephone number to make sure, he lived deep in the bush, about eighty kilometres from here. Jim's post round stretched far and he knew the country and who lived out there. I packed the car expecting to stay away for a few days and started out to the small township that Jim had told me about. "It is really isolated out there. Once you get there take a right at the only junction, follow the track for about ten kilometres and his house is the only one you will come across. I haven't delivered out there for months. He lives on the edge of a tribal area."

I drove for two hours; the road was little more than a track in places. I reached the town, there was a pub, and some rough weatherboard houses. It was on the edge of the

Karri forests and that was where the right turn was. I drove deeper and deeper into the forest. The giant trees enveloped me, I shuddered, I was used to the open spaces. I saw the house, the track dwindled to a path and continued into the trees. I stopped and went up to the front door. I didn't need to knock. Bill walked round from the side of the house. He was in his sixties, he had bright ginger hair which I couldn't take my eyes off and which I'm sure he noticed. I introduced myself and told him the reason I was there.

He asked me in to his house. A tall elegant Aboriginal woman came from the rear of the house. "This is my wife Lorna." We shook hands. "I have a projector, I haven't used it for a long time but we'll try. So you come from the coast? I used to live there but when I came to the forest, I just knew that this is where I wanted to live. You must stay the night."

"Look I don't want to be any trouble, I can sleep in the car." I said.

"No, you must stay here. We'll see if we can make the projector work, and then this evening we'll walk in the forest. I'll introduce you to my friends, Lorna will come with us as our guide. I still get lost after all these years out here. Bill produced the projector, it worked perfectly. He loaded the film, I warned him that I didn't know what to expect. " I don't want to intrude. Once the film is going I'll leave, shout when it comes to an end." Bill left the room. A window looked out to the trees, I could see the sunlight slanting to the ground amongst the colossal trunks.

The film was in colour, and a young man was speaking in English.

"My name is William and I have returned to France and found my parents, Max and Simone. I spent ten years travelling the world. To my shame I never kept in contact with them and since returning I have asked for their forgiveness. Without hesitation they embraced my return, I

couldn't have asked for more, but what was more enlightening ,they wanted to know my story. I wanted to visit places where the wild was dominant and I found such a place in an immense mountain area of South America. There were few people just one uncontacted tribe. They had an ability to reach heights of consciousness I could never have imagined. Their debating skills and thoughts were of a quality that appeared to be of another epoch, far beyond anything that we can manage. They didn't have a word for war. They had no god, they took all their bodily and mental sustenance from their surroundings.

When I left these people, I was sworn to secrecy, I wasn't to write or speak of them. I have allowed myself this one indulgence for you Mum, Dad, for Raimund and you Jack."

I sat up. Why was I included? I saw the film to the end which had scenes of the Alps with Max and Simone, the flowered meadows. I called out to Bill when the film was finishing, he came in and switched it off.

I stayed the night with Bill and Lorna. We went out into the forest . The trees soared over us . Lorna led the way, walking for an hour before meeting her mob and having a brew of tea. On our way back darkness was falling and a wind started to ruffle the tree tops. I was glad I was with somebody, a loneliness could easily creep in if you were out here by yourself.

I left early the next morning. On the journey back I thought about my inclusion in the film. The only explanation was my meeting with Max and Simone and their parting words to me. "Look out for him as you travel across the world."

Driving home through long stretches of undulating country, there were no other cars. Stopping to have a rest, I watched the breeze disturbing the bushes and forming patterns in the grasses. I walked to the back of the car and gazed into the distance, down the road I had driven. A car was approaching, throwing up dust and shimmering in the heat. It was still a long way off. I would let it pass before continuing.

The car stopped, nobody got out. It didn't pull to the side of the road. I had an uneasy feeling and quickly got back into the car and drove. I hated driving fast, this was a moment that I knew I had to get away. I looked in the mirror, nothing, slowing, looking again and I saw the car gaining on me. It was about two hundred metres behind me, two people were in the car. I gripped the wheel, my foot flat on the accelerator, and then it was within metres. It pulled out to overtake, my skill at the wheel was nil, I had no idea of what avoiding action to take.

Forcing me to a halt, I put the car into reverse, but by this time one of the occupants of the car was by my door, opening it and pointing a gun at me. I looked at him, it was the Talker. I got out of the car and barged into him. It was a surprise to me that I did this, and probably him too, he sprawled on the ground, the gun spiralling into the undergrowth. I ran into the bush, it closed around me, I heard a pursuer after me, he tripped and fell heavily, cursing. I let out a roar of laughter as I ducked and dived through the bushes coming to rest among some boulders. This wasn't a time for laughter but the idea that my pursuer was trying to accustom himself to the bush around him gave me pleasure. I was now in control.

I peered out from the boulders and saw the Talker and his companion walking away, back in the direction from where they had come. The Talker was limping badly, and I saw a large snake moving into the undergrowth. I waited for an hour before going back to the road, and when I did I saw that all four tyres on the car had been punctured. I got into the car and slumped. The nearest town was a long way off, few cars used this road and my pursuers might return. While thinking about my next move, I saw a car coming towards me. It was ancient and rattled to a stop beside me. The driver was elderly, he wore a wide brimmed straw hat and as he got out of the car I recognised him immediately. "He told me of his young life in Southern Italy." I had never known his name since it had been a short encounter, but I remembered the sweet strong coffee. He walked to my car, I got out.

"I know you, you stopped at my house a long time ago, you enjoyed my coffee." He put his hand out. "I'm Roberto, I'm making my way to the valleys, they're about ten kilometres from here. I see you have problems. What happened?"

"I went for a walk in the bush and when I got back this is what I found." He didn't believe a word I could see it on his face but I would stay with that story. He offered to take me to the town.

" I don't want to put you to any trouble." I said. He insisted. He then told me about the valleys, his destination. "I go there often, I have built myself a hut, and I'll be staying a couple of days. Why don't you come and visit when you've sorted the car out." I said I might but I needed to get home. After he had dropped me at a garage, he scribbled the directions to the valleys on a piece of paper. I watched him disappear into the distance.

I paid out for the tyres, the lift back to the car and the work and decided to visit Roberto. It was getting late now, I had no food with me so returned to the town, and booked into a pub for the night. I phoned Jessica and told her I would be back in a couple of days.

37

Driving the next morning, always looking for The Talker. The snake may have settled my account with him. I found the turn off for the valleys, the track was little used, slowing me to walking pace on occasions. It was midmorning when I found Roberto's hut. It was set back in a grove of gum trees and when he heard the car, he came out and welcomed me .He wanted me to stay the night, saying that he was going to meet a friend who lived in the valleys. He made me lunch from the many tins he had stored and then the sweet black coffee.

We talked after the meal. "I come here to listen and look. The country is full of birds and animals. People don't have time to listen and look. That's how I met my friend Erijol. I was sitting over in one of the other valleys. I heard slight noise in the bush and saw him padding quietly towards an outcrop of rocks which overlook a stream. We saw each other at the same time. We've become good friends, he knows the country well. His community is a long way off, he leaves to be alone, and now and again comes my way. He should be arriving soon and then we'll walk and go to the caves."

Roberto showed me to a small room in his hut where I could sleep. "There's a spring at the back, that's your washing place!"

Erijol arrived and when I saw him there was a faint moment of recognition, but I couldn't say why. He was old and gnarled and shook my hand for ages with a wide beam on his face which had his life lined through it. I felt an intense calm when I looked into that face. "We must start for the caves, there are only a few hours of daylight." Roberto said. It didn't take us long and when I saw them the feeling of having been there before was strong. The rock art was the dreaming all those years before with Raimund on the coast. I then looked at Erijol. He was Plin and Tub. We moved deeper into the caves. Roberto showed me bones of animals now long extinct.

We returned to the hut and as the sun set we listened to the night sounds starting. Erijol moved off into the scrub. He had a sleeping place among the rocks. We sat out until after midnight, the moon picking out the landscape. It was quiet except for scuttling and a night bird in the distance. I asked Roberto about his family, at first reluctant, but then he started to tell me about leaving Italy.

"I never married. When I arrived here, I walked as far from the world as possible and that meant into the desert. Jack I had been through the war. I couldn't face the stupidity of our species. The killing had appalled me. To a certain extent I didn't want anything else to do with human kind. In the desert I found peace. I met people of the same mind, Europeans and Native Australians. I did meet a Russian woman, who had been through the siege of Stalingrad. She was a wonderful person. We started a school, it must have been the most isolated school. Our pupils were Aboriginal children and children of those who had come to work in the desert townships. We had no more than twenty five pupils. You know the authorities got to hear of the school and because we weren't following what was laid down by the government, it was closed down. It ran for seven years and I heard that many of the pupils went on to higher education. Why should people want to stop something that is successful?"

" Svetlana, that was her name, was killed in a car accident, she was heavily pregnant with our baby. So since then I have tilled my small plot of land where you first met me, travelled in the desert collecting artefacts lying around and taking them to museums."

Roberto's story was of a life of sadness, regret and then hope. He carried with him the consequences of war, he tried to throw it off but the memories were stark, and that was his reason for seeking solace in the desert. And I think he did. I often visited Roberto in his hut in the valleys and at his house on the highway. He wrote a book about his encounters in the valleys. It was a book that described the country he knew in minutiae. There were descriptions of copses, boulders, trees, animals, animal trails, the seasons, the people. When I saw him in the valleys he melted into the bush, he moved with such care for the surrounding plants and animals. His footsteps were light and considerate although he was in a harsh unforgiving place.

He had grown up in Southern Italy and had two brothers and two sisters. His father had been a farmer who supplied the villages with cheeses and milk from his flock of goats. His mother was a brave woman who stood up to the local Mafia and was a member of the local council. When the war came, Roberto together with other young men in the village were forced to join the army. He was sent to Northern Italy and from there to Austria, coming into contact with the German army. His regiment was scorned by the Germans. They were seen as ill disciplined, unfit to fight, but most of all inferior to their counterparts who were members of an SS regiment.

After many months in Austria they were moved all over Italy to fill the gaps as the advance of the British and Americans became unstoppable. He witnessed the slaughter of hundreds of his fellow soldiers. Roberto fled the battlefield and made his way back to his home. None of his family had survived, the retreating German army had destroyed and killed. The family farm was a wasteland. He remained in Italy for a year after the war and then using his wits, sailed in ships to reach Australia. He was twenty when he arrived and he made for the wilderness.

He was transformed by what he found. The silence was the great healer for him. The sound of gunfire, machines, the jabber of voices were absent. He immersed himself in his surroundings, building a shelter, learning hunting skills from tribal people who he encountered deep in the desert.

After two years he suddenly left the wilderness. He wanted to try and live again in the world of noise. Embarking on a ship to the west coast of America, he signed on as a deckhand. His gentleness and sobriety were the subject of ridicule on the ship where toughness and hard drinking in the off duty hours were expected. The voyage across the Pacific was an open book to him which he relished, absorbing the experiences of the people on the islands, almost untouched by our ways. He was often to be found in his cabin, which was little more than a shared space with fifteen other crew. He documented the things he saw, the islands, the diversity of people from island to island, the topography. He wrote about it all, and years later it was published.

The descriptions were better than any photograph. They were woven with such care that you could see the skies, hear the water, feel the crowds, smell the jungle. Renowned authors heaped praise on his descriptive writing, but the book was shunned. Roberto wondered why, and had an idea that the differences and the strangeness he recorded were at odds with how people thought now. It frightened and upset their lives.

The ship arrived in San Francisco where he lived for a year. He started to write poetry, travelling through California to festivals, giving readings of his work. Poetry and verse on war of which Roberto had a deep knowledge, his time living in the desert and the voyage across the Pacific. He also lived in Monterey and from there explored the coast, always writing. His papers with his ideas and thoughts were brought together and another book was published. This time criticism on how the Native Americans had been treated got him deported back to Australia.

Living in the desert again, Roberto was seen by tribes people and other desert dwellers walking the grasslands, sitting for hours, writing, returning to his shelter late in the evenings. The shelter had been extended and a crude water system had been constructed feeding off a spring which he shared with others passing by. Sometimes leaving the area for weeks, it was believed he had bought a house near the highway and there had cultivated a garden, but always returning to his antique land.

Erijol was an Aboriginal elder who happened upon Roberto while he was walking his tribal land. The circumstances surrounding the meeting were talked about often. Roberto had become completely lost, something which he wouldn't admit to, but that was Erijol's interpretation. Short of water, no food, he had been wandering for days attempting to find his way back to the shelter. Erijol was sitting on a rock watching this strange figure groping among the rocks and thorn bush looking for a familiar land mark to guide him back to his shelter. From that time Erijol and Roberto became friends. Erijol showed him the desert, they walked the valleys, the gullies, the hills, Roberto an attentive pupil, always making notes.

At first Erijol never went into Roberto's hut, but as time went on and their friendship became closer, he was invited in. He felt that there was something in there that Roberto guarded closely. Roberto was an artist and the back room of the hut was covered with pictures. There were pictures of flowers, animals, insects, and vast canvasses of the country , on shelves were his poetry and writing, clumped together in tatty, disordered piles of paper.

Roberto stayed for longer periods in the valleys, very rarely visiting his house on the highway. He asked me if I was passing it, to look in and make sure that everything was well. "Please walk the house Jack, I have things there that I am very fond of, I should really bring them here." And I did when I was next that way. I pulled into the same layby as I had years before. It was early afternoon, the sun glistened on the corrugated roof. Walking to the door I looked over to the garden and saw an elderly Aboriginal lady watering the vegetables. She saw me and raised her hand in greeting. " I didn't know somebody looked after the garden." I said walking up to her.

"I live up the highway, I know when he is away, he likes me to look after the garden." She said. I told her how I knew Roberto and that he wanted me to check the house, holding up the key. I left her to the watering and went into the house. I was aware of the silence on entering and saw in front of me, in the hall, a portrait of a beautiful young woman. I stood and looked, moving closer and reading a small plaque on the frame. "Svetlana 1952." A life brought to a tragic end.

Looking at another picture, the background seemed familiar. The landscape was wild and continuing to look, I was drawn into it. A gathering of tribal people celebrating. Where was it? When was it? It didn't matter, the singing, the total abandonment in the dance, the chanting filled the land. The movement, the sound. I was suddenly brought back to the moment by the gardening lady. "I can see you listen." She said. Looking at her, not knowing what she meant but at the same time knowing exactly.

"I met Roberto when he came here sixty years ago, I know him well. He understood the ways, he's a good man, and Svetlana was a listener. She loved the wilderness. Her death was a tragedy. We gave her a tribal burial in the valleys and you know sometimes members of her family travel from Russia to visit her grave but that has almost stopped, they were getting very old, I imagine many of them are dead now. I must finish the garden. See me before you go." And at that she left to resume her gardening.

Walking from room to room, the house was full of Roberto's collections, stones, twisted branches, photographs scattered on tables, books, everything had a place, and had been placed with care, but at the same time carefree, as if a child had created a trove. A photograph in the sitting room, Roberto with his Mother and Father? And beside it Roberto with a man I recognised, the name escaped me. There was one last room to check before leaving, it was locked. I searched for a key. Was I intruding? But he did tell me to check the house. Finding a key on a table under the picture of Roberto and his parents, I tried it in the door, it opened. The room was in darkness, a musty smell. The light from the hallway guided me to the curtains, which I drew back and then turned looking into the room. On the wall opposite the window an enormous picture in oils covered the entire space. From floor to ceiling.

A face looked out, a young Roberto, grim and fatigued, dressed as a soldier, companions around him. The countryside was scorched, the few buildings, blackened and ruined. He was holding a gun, his uniform soiled, a belt of ammunition hung loosely over a shoulder. I went closer. Every object and person in the picture had been ravaged by war. The other faces showed strain and fear, they had been brutalised and beaten.

I heard movement in the passage outside the room, the lady came in. We both stood, staring at it in silence. After minutes I looked across to her, she had tears in her eyes. "I have seen it before, it always makes me feel this way." She said. "I know nothing of that war but I want to scream with rage when I look at it. I must go now, when you see Roberto tell him the sweet potatoes are doing well." She smiled and left. I drew the curtains, and quietly left, closing and locking the door, putting the key back on the table. I passed through the living room on my way to the front door and looked again at the photographs on the wall. The man with Roberto, I searched my memory for a name. 'Cannery Row'. Roberto's time in Monterey. I smiled, the depth of Roberto's life made me shudder with satisfaction.

38

I visited the house again months later after having been to see Roberto. The lady was there tending the garden. I greeted her, went into the house and checked the rooms. Before leaving and while sitting on the veranda, she came and sat with me. 'He came out and visited our mob fifteen years ago. He said it was like walking on wealth when he was in the country. He remained for weeks, talking to us, walking with us, watching our ceremonies and when he had been with us for a while, Roberto produced paint brushes, paints, paper. He painted the country and then painted us. They were wonderful, and captured our life completely. Those paintings are now with the elders of the mob who watch over them. They are displayed among the rocks and trees."

Roberto stayed at the shack one time. He walked the beaches with his painting gear. I told Joe about the paintings and one evening picked Joe up in the car to come and look at them. I left the car some distance from the shack and we walked. I always loved that part of the dunes and knew a little used path that eventually came out on to the beach and then it was only a short walk to the shack, as we got nearer I heard music, it was early evening and the sun was dipping towards the sea, the air was still, looking at the shack, I saw Jessica and Roberto sitting on the veranda, glasses in their hands filled with wine, the murmur of conversation, the crackle of laughter. We stopped and looked at this scene, I felt there was nowhere else I would rather be.

We clattered up the stairs and went to the veranda, glasses of wine placed in our hands. We talked, ate, looked at Roberto's pictures. The telephone rang, I answered it. A one way conversation. "OK we'll look at the television, I'll be in touch," returning to the table, avoiding eye contact, Roberto said, "I know what the conversation was about Jack." I was startled. Roberto started to walk the room slowly and then spoke ."The war sucked the life out of the world. It caused rage, agony, helplessness. We must never return to that, but there are forces willing the world to return to that calamity."

" When I fled the battle field I came across a German soldier, he was petrified by what was happening around him. Although I had been fighting alongside the German regiment that the soldier belonged to, I had never spoken to him, did not know his name, I vaguely recognised him. He was cowering in the undergrowth, tears streaked his face, he was calling for his mother. Kneeling to offer comfort and as I did so, a shell landed near us and the shrapnel sliced him in half. He had shielded me from certain death. I grabbed his identity tag and ran. After the war and before reaching these shores, I searched for the family of this soldier. Having his identity tag, and making enquiries at military offices made my search much easier. His home was on the Baltic coast and it was six months after the war had ended when I knocked on the door of a modest house in a village overlooking The Baltic."

"A woman in her forties came to the door. She looked weighed with sadness. I introduced myself and followed her into a sitting room. She stood looking at me with sunken eyes. We talked for hours. My German was quite good having mixed with German soldiers. Simon, her son was eighteen when he was killed that day. It had been a month before she knew what had happened to him, she had been told about her husband Frank the next day. He had been pressed into service to defend Berlin during the advance of the Russians. He was fifty three when he was killed. Simon was her only child."

"When I left her I felt an emptiness that stayed with me for many years. I wrote her a letter when I arrived in Australia and was surprised to receive one in reply. From then on we kept in contact over the years, then the letters stopped. I have kept all the letters and sometimes look at one, it gives me comfort to know she fought against the odds to live. She would have been very old when the letters stopped. Her name, it was Gabriella. I painted a picture of her from memory, it's at the house on the land. I just hope she found some peace during her life, but I doubt it. Need I say anything else about my feelings and emotions when war is an ever present burden upon the world?" Silence, I filled our glasses and was about to speak, Roberto lifted his hand to stop me and said "Let me Jack."

Driving back from Joe's house, I thought to myself, "How can this be, again?"

I drove Roberto back to his house on the highway. We left early, and I promised him that I would visit him on his land. On my return I took diversions to look at landscapes I had known. I arrived back at the shack, got out of the car and climbed the stairs to the front door. It was locked, I fumbled for my keys, unlocked the door. Going in I saw an envelope on the floor. Lucia had arrived in Perth and Jessica had gone to meet her. "She says she has news that we need to know about." Raimund was on the move again, those wanting him destroyed were making every effort to find him.

They had found his island, he had left before their arrival and in haste. His house had been destroyed along with his belongings. Many of the islanders who had helped him had been slaughtered. There were few safe places for Raimund. Lucia thought that he had returned to Greece and to his house on Syros. His publications had infuriated the powerful, they must be stopped and Raimund assassinated.

Roberto had walked away, Raimund was tumbling headlong into the storm. I had to see him again. With Jessica's blessing I started out again to find him.

39

On the beach there were a few people packing up and heading for home after a day's surfing, or just being out beside the ocean. The wind had dropped, the water was still. I had walked about two hundred metres from the shack and looked back. An ideal place to have lived and to have raised the children. Raimund had come to dominate again. There was a strong sense that this may be the last time I would see Raimund. I returned to the shack, had something to eat and then went to bed.

I dreamt. It wasn't about Raimund, it was about William and his return to his parents in Briancon. He had amassed a lot of knowledge while travelling, especially in South America. He was speaking to an audience about what he had learnt. Nobody listened, they laughed at him, he continued, the audience became hostile and some of them approached the rostrum, ripped the microphone out of his hand and wrestled William to the ground, the rest of the audience then approached him and pulled him apart. They held his head high, all screaming with laughter.

I jerked awake, fretting, my body streaming with sweat. Looking into the darkness, imagining figures. Switching on the light I was alone. I got up and went to the veranda, gulping in the sea air. My mind felt bruised. A need to run, but where to? Leaping down the stairs to the beach I ran to the sea's edge, stopped, looked back and then plunged into the dark warm water. I floated, the mass of stars, I looked across to the setting moon. I didn't sleep when I returned. I rang Joe although it was only five. He knew I was leaving, but the need to speak to somebody was urgent, the dream was still driving me.

I went to the car and drove fast. The bus from the main road wasn't for another hour, I left the car for Joe to pick up. I had to be with other people, but when others started to arrive at the bus stop they took on images of a laughing mob. Had I lost my senses? Then calm, I slumped on a seat and cried. The bus arrived, I boarded, looked straight ahead, not catching an eye. I slept for the four hours to the airport.

I never found Raimund. His house on Syros had been sold. I was met with silence to my questions. Nobody on the island would even say that they had known him, fear was crashing down on those who had. I was avoided when I tried to find answers and was advised to leave. I made a pretence of leaving, determined to find somebody who would talk to me. I went to the ferry and slipped away into the crowds. I found a small tavern on the edge of town, and paid for a week's stay.

Hiring a scooter I went to Raimund's house. It was deserted, looking through the windows the rooms were bare. I tried the doors. I was certain the clue to his disappearance was in the house. Walking to the front, I scanned the countryside, to the sea, the pine forests above, and noticed a small chapel hidden in the trees far up the hillside. I had never noticed it before. Nobody was about so I forced a window and climbed in. I searched and went to his writing room. The only thing left in the house was the picture of Hospadyr's funeral in Ethiopia. It was on the wall of the writing room. Why should that have been left? I lifted it off the wall and saw writing on the plaster. "It is the night before I am taken."

The bleating of goats alerted me and walking to the front, I saw an old goatherd tending his flock. I climbed out of the window where I had entered the house and went to the old man. He rattled away and gave a directional nod to the chapel in the trees and then walked off with the goats down the slope. The secrecy of being on the island had probably been compromised but I was intent on finding Raimund.

The climb to the chapel was steep and on reaching it the view to the sea was intriguing in that the town was now hidden by a headland and the house was the only sign of habitation. The door to the chapel was unlocked, the cool interior was welcoming. I sat on a pew for several minutes looking around and noticed evidence of somebody having slept near the altar. There was a drape and a hassock which had been used as a cover and a pillow lying on the floor. Stepping outside I walked around the chapel and then started walking up through the pines to a scree slope. It got steeper, and became a rough path leading to the summit. A figure stood out among the boulders dressed in a red jacket far up the mountain. I shaded my eyes, it must be Raimund. The figure stopped, looked my way, raised an arm and waved. He disappeared through the boulders.

That evening I waited in the chapel for his return. He didn't come back. Soon after midnight, picking my way carefully, I returned to the scooter and went back to the tavern.

Thumping on my room door woke me, looking at my watch, it was six o'clock. Three men entered the room, one was The Talker, his companion, and a brute with an American accent. The Brute dominated, his hands on his hips. "Your friend Raimund is a fraud, everything he has told you is a lie. Now what I suggest you do is fuck off back to your beach and stay there. Your faggot friends in Berlin are a warning." He thrust a picture at me. I saw Jurgen and Joseph bound with rope. He snatched it back, the three turned to leave and as they did, I said to the Talker, "I hope the next snake does a better job." He faced me, a fist raised,

The Brute caught him by the collar and threw him through the door. I heard their footsteps disappearing. The lady owner appeared at the door shaken. I packed, not looking, stumbled out of the tavern to the port and caught a ferry to the mainland.

40

Doubt had been sown. "Raimund is a fraud." I would prove otherwise. I returned to the beach. Jessica refused to leave on anymore travels. Lucia felt the same. "I know he is my brother Jack, the time has come to stop pursuing Raimund. He must see to himself now."

I started out to find Raimund. I gave myself two months. "He's in Spain Jack. He went to the city of Seville. He got in touch with us when he had left Greece. He told us should you be looking for him go to an address that has a street painting of Groucho Marx on the wall outside. That was all he told us. When you have found him, come to us and stay on your way home, I want you to meet William." Max ended the conversation by wishing me luck.

The train arrived in the early evening from Madrid. I walked to the city centre and found a small guest house. It had been a lot of travelling. A meal and bed were the only things that interested me. I slept long into the morning, so long that the manager came to see if I was alright.

I ambled the streets looking out for Groucho Marx and then on the second day I found the painting in a narrow street that led to one of the squares. I stood back from the building expecting Raimund to appear. I rang the bell. A boy opened the door, I said "Raimund." It was totally inadequate but my knowledge of Spanish was inadequate. He went back into the house and then a woman appeared. She looked severe, I said "Raimund." She turned and went back in. Then a man came to the door, a jovial round face, he clasped me with both hands and said, "Jack we have been expecting you, Raimund is here, come in." We walked down a long corridor, I could hear Raimund's voice. Up a flight of stairs to a room with a terrace leading to a view of the city. Raimund was standing, he was using his mobile phone, he ushered me over and squeezed my arm, gesturing that he would be a few more minutes and that I should sit down until he had finished.

Looking round the room, my gaze fell on a picture over the fireplace. I got up and walked over to it. It was a picture of Don Quixote. One of the books Joe, me and Jessica didn't finish while on our quest to understand Raimund. Quite suddenly something in my mind joined up the years of knowing him. The similarity was eerie and thinking back on the book, the part I did read was familiar with the person standing in the room speaking on a mobile phone. When he had finished, he stood beside me looking at the picture. He didn't say anything, then "Come Jack to the terrace." We walked out into the brilliant sunlight and looked out across the city. It was late morning, the street sounds and a slight breeze reached us.

I told Raimund about my trip, the days on Syros looking for him, The Talker and The Brute, the capture of Jurgen and Joseph, Max and Groucho Marx. "Was that you on the hill above your house in Syros?" I said.

"Yes it was and the two you talk about had found my home, I left in haste, staying the night in the Chapel. I'm sorry I didn't welcome you, my life was hanging then. They stripped my house of everything and made a pyre of all my belongings further down the mountain."

I asked about Jurgen and Joseph. "They were taken by people who support the destruction of art and literature, these people want to destroy and start a society subservient to their dismal way of thinking. But what I have heard is that Joseph and Jurgen escaped. They escaped when being transported to a camp and are making their way here. Crossing the Pyrenees by foot. It sounds like Mother and Dad all those years ago. Anyway Jack you have travelled from the other side of the world again. You didn't have to do it."

"Raimund, how long have we known each other? Twenty years? I'm going to quote something to you for once." He laughed

"Cicero, Raimund, he wrote. "Friendship is something that unites the human and the divine, friendship is to have someone to tell everything to, give hope and do not bend before destiny. Someone with whom to share good luck and bad luck." We need it more than ever in a world that has become cruel. Friendship remains the most precious asset."

I stayed in Seville only to make sure that Raimund was safe. I never knew why I felt compelled to do this, it was more than friendship, it was about being with somebody who was deeply part of me, his ideas, enthusiasms, his mischievous ways, his knowledge, his opposition to the wreckers and grabbers, and his respect for the elemental.

We walked the streets of Seville, went to the country, met his friends, drank with them, discussed and argued. I was reminded of this Don Quixote figure on my lone ramblings out of the city. He gave me a map and directions of where I should visit. The ancient churches, villages ,towns. I saw a deep feeling of belonging that the people had for the land. Vineyards, woods, homesteads. I was reminded of Leonardo, his search for the best wood for his guitars. Returning each evening, Flamenco filled the air.

I left this world which was clinging for survival and returned to the shack. I kept up with Raimund over the months. I knew that he wasn't an enthusiast for modern communications, his letters kept me informed. I also used to phone Lucia, I felt that she had lost interest, she was now elderly, but was always pleased to hear from me.

I visited Roberto on the land. He never wanted to know what was happening on the outside. He had his garden, his hut in the wilds. Joseph and Jurgen made it to Seville. They opened a coffee bar, and in a back room they had a small printing press, where they kept the memory of Marianne alive by producing the satire which she was so well known for. Although living openly Raimund was never exposed. He fitted his surroundings and nobody asked questions. I saw Max, Simone and William on the way home. William told me about meeting Raimund. The depth of his life had influenced his thinking, and he took from their conversations ideas which he thought he could develop and practise in his own life and pass to others.

41

Then as has happened on many occasions a long letter arrived from Raimund, it had been sent special delivery. It was typed which I was glad of, since most of his letters were in long hand and his writing was difficult to understand. I didn't rush to read it, I needed quiet and a calm sunlit day. I chose a day when Jessica was out, the fishing could wait and when I knew Joe was out on the boat. I had a supply of coffee and a view of the ocean.

My dear Jack and Jessica. I have found where I want to remain for my days. Xlia has joined me. I have kept the old house in Colombia. An old friend is going to live there. Zania is staying on in Colombia. I never told you she has four daughters. Since you left I have continued my wanderings in the country and have been to other cities. I now keep a diary and am taking photographs again. I have a feeling for this country. I know of Spain's conquests and the terrible hardships people endured, especially on my continent.

I found myself in a cloistered church in the mountains of Madrid. It had been built since the conquests and around the cloisters were many portraits in the stonework. My eye was caught by one particular portrait, that of a man in modern dress. In the background was evidence of war and desolation, he stared out with a sense of calm on his face. That face was telling me that although the world was at war, peace, understanding and acceptance would prevail. The face was of Old Hazard . I remember you telling me of Hugo's film and that Old Hazard had fought in the Spanish civil war and had been with the partisans in the fascist war. But to find his portrait on a cloister near Madrid was a surprise. I wanted to find out the reasons behind this.

I found the priest whose church it was and asked him. He said that he didn't know but I knew very well that he did. I returned to the church one night with a torch. I felt the reason for Old Hazard's portrait lay within. The church wasn't locked. That calm face in the stonework contradicted my findings. Old Hazard had written a diary. It was in a drawer near the altar. I read it, my torch gradually fading, until streaks of dawn appeared in the stained glass windows. It was his life, the war and predictions. Those predictions were chilling. I keep them to myself because I am determined that they won't succeed. Remember he was a Shaman and he had an insight. Thoughts, actions, ideas can change, even those of a shaman. I still respect Old Hazard although he was filled with doom for the future.

Leonardo came to see me. We talked about our captivity and made it one of our aims to force governments to face up to the disappearances which are still occurring, carried out by rogue elements. I know I am being sought. They won't find me and I will continue to have my work published with the help of Joseph and Jurgen –

The day was closing when I finished the letter. It was the last time I heard from Raimund. I tried to contact him, there was no response. Lucia had died. I went to Melbourne and saw the neighbour. He told me that he hadn't seen her for several days and when he went to the house, he found her dead in the living room, sitting in a chair. On her lap there was an open photograph album. There were six photographs, all of the family in Argentina taken many years ago. Raimund stands in the centre of one of them. Raimund a fraud? A person I had accompanied on many of his quests. I was a witness, he was never a fraud. Unusual, a mischief maker, a dissenter, a deep thinker about what we are and where we are heading.

The neighbour handed me some papers in an envelope with an attached letter. "Jack, I've left this for you. I wanted you to know about some of the deeds that Raimund partook in when he first arrived in Europe. He recorded everything in diaries. I have picked out a few of the events and hope you get pleasure out of reading about them. The diaries are in a depository box in Berlin, Marianne knew where they were, but now that she is dead, Joseph and Jurgen might know the location of that box. If you have time tell The King of Spain about the prison breakout! Lucia." I didn't start reading the papers until I got back to the shack and when I had finished I realised that there was much more to know. But I knew enough, if I should ever find the diaries of course I would read them, but I was happy with what I knew about Raimund. For the moment!

42

And this is what I read.

Europe, Raimund tramped for months, starting in the far west of the Iberian Peninsula, Portugal. A country that mariners had set sail from across the oceans, plundering, conquering, amassing wealth. Dictators had brutalised people, yet how he loved the country. Why was it that despots had ruled for centuries? The same could be said for most of the countries of that continent. Destroyed and pillaged by war for thousands of years, and now the green shoots of freedom, for how long?

While meandering on the banks of The Douro, he saw a dog running loose on the gravelly track, a short time later a middle aged woman appeared from the trees carrying a bunch of flowers. Raimund's Portuguese was not good but he understood that she was looking for her dog. He pointed down the road. Realising his difficulty with the language she changed to Spanish. The dog appeared and ran towards them, panting and scuffling in and out of the undergrowth.

"I've been looking for him, he is naughty. When he disappears he always goes and visits my husband's grave, although he never knew him. There's some kind of sense there." He was taken aback by the woman divulging this information but she said it with such warmth in her voice that it was a signal to indulge in further conversation with her. They walked to a low building set back from the track and went into a graveyard through a metal gate. The graveyard was enclosed by a low drystone wall, and the building was surrounded on all sides by graves, some of them well tended with newly laid flowers. They had been chatting about the day, the countryside, the river which could be seen through the trees, the vineyards hugging The Douro.

"This is where my husband Carlos is, and over there my two brothers, all of them executed by the dictator." She slowly bent down and placed the flowers on the grave. There was a picture of him on the gravestone; he must have been in his thirties. She blew a kiss, then visited the graves of her brothers. He saw her lips moving as if she was saying a prayer, but Raimund noticed that there were no religious symbols anywhere, perhaps she was reciting a poem.

"I know you are a traveller, you must stay the night at my house and refresh, it's still a long way to the Spanish border " He didn't know how she knew his way but she did and he didn't question it. "Come, I must return to the house." They walked through vineyards to an old stone house which overlooked the river. The white house in the intense afternoon sun and then the cool shade of trees was welcome. She walked to the front door and with a large key unlocked it. Raimund followed her into a huge room. There was a stage at one end of the room which was covered with musical instruments. He followed her up a winding staircase where the bedrooms, sitting room, and dining room were. He put his belongings into one of the bedrooms and then followed her downstairs.

They went to the rear of the house, a wide veranda with a view to the vineyards. Raimund and Gabriela talked through the afternoon." My husband, Carlos was a musician, he played the piano and this is where he played. He started an orchestra, he felt the need to bring quiet to people who were living through those times and in this house he accomplished that. He was a wonderful man, musicians from all over the country and beyond wanted to support him. He was a pacifist and at the time the colonial wars in Africa were raging. He refused to be taken to the army. The generals were aware of his following and strangely left him alone." Gabriela stopped talking and went to answer the door, saying "I think it must be Maria, she said she would prepare a meal for us."

"I don't want to be a nuisance you know."

"You're not a nuisance. I've just finished a book about Carlos. I would like you to have a copy. When I was putting the flowers on his grave today, I somehow felt that you should know about him. This evening you must tell me about yourself." He was humbled when Gabriela told him this but since starting his journey he had met people who were willing to tell him about themselves and out of these ordinary stories, extraordinary events happened.

The evening he met a shepherd high in the mountains who was making for his shelter. He had lived in the mountains all his life and believed that the birds at night carpeted the earth with music. He said he could hear the music as he nodded to sleep and depending on the music he could tell what the next day would bring. Then there was the peasant woman tending her small orchard who told him that her dog was the reincarnation of her daughter who died at a year old. The dog would lie under the empty crib at night having placed the dead daughter's toys around him before he went to sleep.

"He gathered the orchestra together and as I have said, musicians from all over this country and Spain came to play. They came to this house and the music started. Musicians packed on to the stage, and those who came to listen thronged the floor, the door was left open so those outside could hear. Hundreds sat among the trees on the summer evenings, the music drifted out and over the vineyards."

"They played the classics, jazz, flamenco and of course Fado. It was relief from the terror of those times. Those in the orchestra believed that they would never be touched by the authorities. Carlos was at his height. It lasted for two years; they were wonderful but frightening times. Finally the police started to visit and mingle with the crowds on the orchestral evenings, they played on. He told the musicians that if they wanted to leave because of the attention they were receiving from the police, they could, but not one did.

The lead violinist, Garcia would walk among the crowds especially on the evenings the police were there. They were embarrassed, enraged, they made for the exit. The music destroyed their plans, wasn't that wonderful?"

They dined well that evening. Gabriela continued her story " Carlos was arrested two years after he had started the orchestra. They came to the house one night after a music evening, the audience had gone home. They were brutal, they crashed through the house, smashing the instruments, taking what they wanted, I never saw Carlos again. He was executed days later. My brothers were arrested for their opposition to the regime soon after. My home is my memorial to Carlos, to what happened here, and to what could happen again."

He stayed for two nights, her kindness urged him on. She supplied him with food for the day's walk and just as he was leaving she gave him a picture of her husband in a small silver frame and the book about him. Her parting words. "Keep his memory alive." Climbing the stony path out of the valley he looked back and could see Gabriela with hand raised. Although sadness had invaded her life she refused to allow it to stop her.

Walking high, he looked down on The Douro, tourist boats came into sight on occasions, he waved in greeting, the commentary reaching up to him, and then they disappeared around a bend in the river. Silence was all around him, not a hint of disturbance in the bushes and trees; it had been a perfect morning to have set off. The track led from the vineyards, falling to the river, into quiet woods, the sun piercing the canopy and striking the ground in front of him. The food Gabriela had supplied was a feast along with a bottle of wine. He sat staring out over the countryside, a herd of goats far in the distance being guided through a field gate.

Time to continue on his way, he had finished most of the

wine, the distances flew passed. Late afternoon, but still no sign of the village where he hoped to spend the night, a bend in the river and there it was. It would be two more days to the Spanish border. Arriving in the village, the curious stares, the smiles, the glum faces. He saw the inn sign; he went in and was greeted warmly by the owner, Gonzales. His room overlooked the main street. It had been a tiring day; he kicked off his boots and collapsed on the bed. An hours rest was what he needed.

He was woken by the sound of a band and revelry in the street below his window. Looking out, the street was a mass of celebrating people. A slow procession was ambling, led by about ten musicians, clad in remarkable outfits, masks propped on their heads. When the music stopped they pulled the masks over their faces, a sinister grouping emerged. The swaying parade reached the square, silence, then slowly they put the masks back on top of their heads, readied their instruments and music filled the streets.

Raimund hurried from his room down to the square and joined the laughing clapping crowds raising their arms. An energy swept through the street. He wondered about the origin of this gathering and when making his way back to the inn he saw the innkeeper who waved at him and called him over to join his friends, they shook his hand, patted his back.

"It is our way of showing allegiance to life." Gonzales said. "We have been doing it for decades, watch what happens next!" The light had faded and beyond the street the sky was ablaze with stars. The crowds were silent and from the darkness he could hear snuffling and grunting and then pigs charged down the street. Everybody clapped and cheered, the pigs bounded up the alleyways, wherever they wished. Raimund looked at Gonzales quizzically, "Yes our way of showing how grateful we are to them. We allow them to roam anywhere; unlike other villages we don't kill them. They turn the fields, they fertilize, in winter they go to the woods and remain there until spring when they raise their litters. They are very important to us. I love them; each one has a special character."

He pressed on along the banks of The Douro. The Spanish border getting nearer. It was late afternoon when he saw the border post. He was following a little used road but even it had a frontier. Arriving at a hut, two grim looking guards taking in this new arrival. He may well have been the only person to have arrived that day. Producing his passport, one of the guards waved it away. He looked into the hut and saw what would become normal, the ever present picture of the dictator. Franco this time! He was told to go into the hut and both guards seemed to relax when inside. A glimmer of a smile on both their faces. "Sit down, sit down." One of the guards said. He sat at a table, and from a cupboard the guard produced, cheese, bread and wine: *"and kind things done by men with ugly faces."*

Raimund left the border crossing, said goodbye to the river and set his course for Salamanca and then on to Madrid. A car stopped for him, the driver was with her family and was driving to Salamanca. There were two children in the back among the guitars and bags. It was many hours to their destination and during the conversation; Juanita told Raimund that her husband had been in prison for five years, a prisoner of the regime. He was in a notorious prison in Madrid. He had been a film producer and when one of his films portraying Franco as an empty headed aristocratic oaf, he was swept up and away to prison.

They arrived in the city late; Juanita said that Raimund must stay the night before travelling on. They talked into the night, the children asleep, and from that conversation he found out where the prison was. It was a time in his journey when Raimund felt the need for resistance to the stifling conformities that surrounded the times. He contacted an old friend of his from Chile who had fled the regime there. He wasn't sure of her intentions, fleeing one dictator only to find herself in a country of another. Her name was Helena. Remember Raimund was naïve, impatient, idealistic. He knew that Mother and Dad had been in Spain in the early day of Franco's rule. They had spoken a lot of their time there and he had always wanted to see the places they spoke of.

43

He found the prison where Juanita's husband Solo was and that is when he started to plan. He stayed with Helena and told her about Juanita and Solo and the idea of trying to help him escape. "Raimund, you cannot possibly do that, if you are caught the consequences will be dire. You will be executed when they catch you. This country is full of whispers, trust is difficult to come by, you will need people to help you, you'll never do it by yourself."

"Will you help me Helena?" Her mouth fell open," I can trust you, we've known each other for a long time." A long silence.

"I need to think Raimund, it is late now, let's sleep and I'll give you an answer in the morning."

They started to plan, Helena seemed to be an expert, she just smiled when he asked her about her knowledge of prison escapes. "I will tell you sometime." They spent days working out what they should do. Visiting the street where the prison was, watching those entering and leaving. Who should he take the part of? The priest, too obvious, a visitor, there weren't any. They watched a side entrance, cooks, prison guards, people working in administration, and then they noticed a young man entering the prison each day carrying what appeared to be wood working tools. The café from where they watched was often populated by guards, before and after their shifts, brutal looking men who had no time to talk.

The carpenter was their target and Helena would display her charms. They were in the café when he was approaching the prison. Helena walked towards him, entwined an arm around his and guided him to the café. "Juan, how are you? I haven't seen you for a long time."

"But I'm not Juan,"

"You are today, come, have a drink with us." A drink was put in front of him.

"I must get to work. " Protesting this intrusion.

"Haven't you heard? Franco is dead, the prison is closed," and then a vast parade entered the street, music, street performers, acrobats, fire eaters, clowns. Crowds gathered, cheering and clapping. The off duty guards were gathered into the parade. Their faces wondering but now breaking into abandonment, the gates of the prison opening. "What's happening?" Banners unfurling – Franco is dead – Fear in the eyes of those officials looking out, guards deserting. Raimund grabbed the carpenter's tools and entered the gates. Orders had ceased but anybody shouting out a request or command was obeyed, "Open the cells." Raimund shouted. Nobody questioned him, he must be an official, but he's only young. It doesn't matter, he gave an order. Solo walked out and away, as they all did and nobody in authority asked. Questions, recriminations, but somebody said," Open the cells." To this day nobody knows. "Flee Solo, leave Spain, Juanita and the children are waiting for you in France."

Raimund left Madrid and headed for the Pyrenees. Helena stayed and Solo reached his family in France. The laughter echoed around Spain. The walking had exhausted him and when he arrived in the mountains, he found refuge with a shepherd and his wife. They owned a small hut beside their house where he stayed. They invited him in to share their food . He accompanied the shepherd on some days, walking the mountains, tending the sheep.

Resting in their house one evening and looking at the photographs displayed on a table near the fire place, his attention was drawn to a group of four people standing outside the house. Picking it up he saw Mother and Dad staring out. Pierre, the shepherd came into the room and said, "My mother and father, the other two were travelling to Madrid from France, it was about 1936. My father used to talk about them when I was young. He said that the man used to act and sing in the evenings, and that the lady had quite wonderful costumes that she wore. The locals would come to the house from the villages to watch the performances." Raimund nodded and smiled, to be in the house where Mother and Dad had been many many years before was the most satisfying feeling.

He walked into France and along the Mediterranean coast. It was September and he had been on his journey for four months. His progress came to a halt one morning near Marseilles. A police car pulled up in front of him.

"Raimund Roello?" The officer enquired. He didn't know how to react to this, the Madrid prison was uppermost in his mind, surely not. Raimund produced his passport and showed it to the officer, "You must come with me Mr Roello, there is a woman who would like to speak to you."

" But who? I've done nothing since entering France, so please – "

" Mr Roello, get into the car." Raimund walked to the car and got into the back.

"I want to know what this is about?"

They drove fast leaving the motorway, a minor road, a rough track, passed vineyards, waterfalls from what was now mountain country. They stopped outside a remote bar and that is where he met Marianne and her husband Victor.

Of course you know that Marianne was Raimund's publisher and this was to be their first meeting. Victor kept in the background. Raimund found out that Victor's father had helped his mother and father to perform in Berlin before the war. Solo, who had been freed from the Madrid prison had set this meeting up. Marianne was fascinated to meet the person who had engineered such an astonishing act. The friendship grew from there.

His mother and father's reputation was well known in France, Spain and Germany. There had been, and still is a long history of satire, the Roello name was connected with it. The Madrid prison was discussed and relished. You know the bar still exists and is a meeting place for satirists. He gained in strength from the meeting and that is the Raimund you see today.

Once he returned to the Spanish side of The Pyrenees, to the place where his mother and father had crossed. He was risking his liberty because of the prison breakout in Madrid. Let the diary tell you about his life during those months.

I stayed with a family on their farm in one of the valleys. I had got to know the family because the old grandfather remembered Mother and Dad. I knew I was safe, few people passed that way. There was one regular visitor, an Irish woman called Sinead. She lived in a neighbouring village. Sinead was a doctor and had left Ireland when she was twenty five. She spoke fluent Spanish and practised as a doctor in the villages to which she rode on a mule. She sang when she rode and the villagers would gather on the heights on her approach, to listen. The songs were a mix of Irish ballads, opera, and Spanish folk traditions. Her voice was wonderful.

I stayed in the mountains for six months. Sinead was my lover. I was enchanted by her. The way she embraced the life of this part of Spain, the people, their traditions, the history. I loved her for all sorts of reasons. And then she disappeared. At first people said that she had returned to Ireland. I felt empty. Throughout our time together I had never visited her house. I hadn't even been to the valley where she lived. Desperate to find out where she had gone, I trekked across the mountains. It was winter and a blizzard was tearing through. I reached the village and found her house. Nobody answered when I knocked on the door. I went to the neighbour.

The neighbour was an elderly lady who told me that the doctor had left and gone to Madrid. When she left, she was with two men. I asked to go into the house and the lady although reluctant at first, handed me a key after I had told her the reasons for my visit. The tidiness inside was uncanny. There was nothing to connect Sinead with the house. I had a feeling that I was in the wrong place, the neighbour insisted that this was where the doctor lived.

I went to the local police, they showed no interest. I talked to other doctors, they were unable to help. It was sinister and disturbing.

I continued my search. I knew a path that dipped down to towns and villages and taking that path, I came to a small town I often visited. A group of men were gathered in the square, talking, drinking, some playing cards, laughter. I approached and on recognising me, they drew me into their circle, poured me a drink from the bottle on the table. At first they didn't speak to me, they were happy I was there, I felt a belonging. They watched the play of the cards and when it had finished, one of them directed his gaze towards me.

"Raimund, we have been waiting for you. We expected you in the winter, but it was a chilling time for travellers and many of the roads were blocked. You must stay now. My friend Zamora will give you lodgings and we will talk over the days about Sinead. She was our doctor in the town and we have a lot to tell you."

I was astonished by this unexpected turn.

"She spoke about you to everybody she came into contact with. Do you see that building over there? It has a stage inside and she used to sing there, quite wonderful singing. You must dine with me this evening, and in the morning we will walk to the waterfall, the place where she was last seen."

I was led away from the group by Zamora, the owner of the town's hotel and shown to a room overlooking the square, the men still sitting, card playing, sipping their drinks, cigarette smoke hovering above them.

"You must be tired, rest, and Carlo will come for you in an hour and take you to eat."

Spanish faces looked down on me from the pictures dotted around the walls. I had an audience. I felt a sense of well-being. Carlo arrived and we walked to a taverna in a street off the square. It was crowded, the laughter was infectious, guitar music rounded the atmosphere. We settled and Carlo told me about Sinead and her abduction. It was uplifting and then chilling. "Sinead was a woman beyond the times. She administered to everybody, especially women and girls. She became more and more concerned about their health. Then there were whispers that she was providing birth control and even performing abortions. The care she offered was outstanding to both men and women."

"Father Emanuel, our local priest heard the whispers. He was a deeply loved man in the town and beyond, a man with ideas other than God. He was a rascal. He had come from another part of Spain, and at first was looked upon with suspicion. He introduced new thinking into this deeply conservative community. It found a home with many people, who before, followed the doctrines of orthodoxy. Not only was the church being challenged but also the medical profession. Spain was not ready for this, if the church was questioned, how long before the government experienced the same?"

"It was best to be rid of the two of them. Sinead spoke of your upbringing in South America. She drew inspiration from this, she also spoke of Ireland and the parallel with Spain, she meant the church and that it must change. Her outspokenness found its way to the ears of government. Her difficulties started."

Carlo stopped speaking while he greeted two women who had entered the taverna. He got up from the table and introduced me. When they left, he said that one had been Father Emanuel's house keeper.

"She was ordered to stop practising. The government was nervous about her because she was a foreigner, but Father Emanuel, there were no such nerves. He was taken and executed. When they searched his house, it was crammed with books, and the most glorious find was a conversation he had with God. He had recorded this in note books."

"I knew one of the civil guards who had taken part in the search. I had known this man for many years. He hated Franco but he stayed in the job because he had a wife and children to feed. I asked him about the note books. They had been hastily taken by the church authorities, first to Madrid and then to Rome I believe. They were seen as blasphemous, disrespectful, profane. The civil guard had seen one and said that it was uproarious. When Father Emanuel asked God, "And was Jesus – ?" It was ripped from his hand by a senior officer. The completed question was on the next page! Oh how I would have loved to have seen those note books. Sinead, she went to Madrid, so if you want to find her you must start there."

I said farewell to Carlo and Zamora and started for Madrid. I knew it was foolish and hoped time had grown over the prison break. I felt confident that my presence in a large city would go unnoticed. I found lodgings in a poor area. My landlady was a gypsy, who had settled in Madrid. She and her husband were musicians. They found me work in a bar where they sometimes played; I worked in the evenings and spent my days searching for Sinead. I had a free evening and walked the streets looking, and then I heard Sinead's voice filling the street. That voice, how could I forget it? Going over to the door from where her voice was coming from, I looked in, the bar was crammed. I pushed through the throng and found a dark recess. It was early, people still came. I listened for nearly an hour, until an interval. Should I approach the manager and ask to speak to Sinead? But before I had made a decision the lights dimmed and she was on the stage again.

As she sang, I looked at the people in the bar. All ages, many Romany faces, the music stopped abruptly. I asked the man beside me what was happening. "This happens sometimes when the Señora is singing. The secret police arrive, disrupt the performance, warn the management, everybody leaves, but it looks like this time it is different."

I saw two men go to Sinead, lead her from the stage, barge her through the crowd to the entrance. I tried to reach her, shouting her name, but she was gone. Returning to where I had been standing, I noticed an elderly couple at a table beside the stage. The woman was weeping, the man holding her arm. The crowd slowly left the bar. I stayed until it was almost empty, and when the elderly couple left, I left. Identities were being checked outside.

I ran, hands tried to grasp me; the advantage was mine, into alleyways, over walls, through backyards, across gardens, hidden in crowds, behind the door of my lodgings, safety. I peered into the dark street from my room, nobody. My landlady arrived home, she called up to me and I joined her in the kitchen. She mentioned that there had been a lot of police in the city. I told her that I had been to the cinema.

Returning to my work, always watching. I had only been

somebody who ran from a bar, why should they be looking? It had been dark outside Sinead's bar; even so, I must take care. On my evening off I returned to see if I could find Sinead. It had been a week since my escape. The streets were quiet. Approaching the bar and hearing her singing I went in, keeping to the shadows. I stood and listened. There was one man sitting among the tables which were set for a feast. As she was finishing a song, the doors opened and people poured in and made for the tables.

The elderly weeping lady and her husband sat near the stage. Sinead's singing filled the room and walking nearer, I saw that her face was bruised and swollen. I slunk back. A group of men were being shown to a table. I watched as they ordered from a waitress. One of them grabbed the waitress and tried to kiss her, she pulled away. The man pointed at her in an accusatory manner, mouthing insults. The waitress moved to my part of the room, I sidled over and asked her who the men were. "Police." She said and quickly moved among the tables. The men stood up, the singing stopped, they surrounded two women at a table, near to where I was standing. They didn't say anything to the women, they took them and left.

I had to leave. I started for the door, looking back at Sinead. She hesitatingly half raised her arm in acknowledgement, she had recognised me, her face questioning. The street was empty, the audience started to leave, the old couple first, and finally Sinead. She saw me, walked over to me, we embraced.

In a café far from Sinead's bar, we talked." When I left the villages I came here. The police threatened me and set me up in the bar where you found me. I knew why they had done this, to entice dissenters. That is what these places do, and once inside they are arrested. If I don't do as they say, I am beaten. You can see the results." She paused.

"They have my passport, I am the bait. I try to warn, but

am being watched all the time. I feel like a collaborator. How can I break free from them?"

I told her about my encounter with Carlo and Zamora. "Yes, they were both wonderful friends. When I had finished my rounds in the villages, our evenings were filled with music and laughter. Father Emanuel often joined us, he was a man of great knowledge and intellect, and brought into question his belief in God. He worked tirelessly for the community and filled the churches with his sermons. Laughter, yes laughter, where there was once poker faced solemnity. The churches in the valleys were places of hilarity. Can you believe it? Laughing with God! This was blasphemy. He questioned the authority of Rome, he criticised the Holy Father, and then he was snatched by the secret police and taken to Madrid."

Sinead was silent; she sipped her drink, tears in her eyes, and then started to tell me more. "He disappeared into nothingness. All enquiries were met with surprise. We've never heard of him: I don't know what you're talking about. It was cruel. A story emerged that he had been garrotted. His family never received a body and to this day nothing is known. There's a little girl in one of the villages who looks just like Father Emanuel. I know you have seen the old couple who come to the bar, they are Father Emanuel's mother and father."

She stopped talking, drank her wine, looking into the distance, passed me, and to the street. "Raimund, I must escape. I have to go by myself; it is too dangerous to be seen with me." I then told her about the prison break. "Then you must definitely not be seen with me. You won't see me again. I have a plan for my escape, even you mustn't know it." She put her hand on mine, got up and left. I watched her go through the door and into the street. I had never felt as sad and alone as at that moment. The café was closing, I got up to leave, went out, and peered into the darkness, hoping Sinead was still in sight, just a gentle breeze rattled the trees. Not a soul. I walked slowly back to my lodgings, passed Sinead's bar. It was closed.

I stayed another two days, told my landlady I was leaving, gave my notice at the bar where I worked. I searched the crowds for Sinead during that time and then left.

He ambled his way through Italy, eventually arriving in Venice, where he remained for six months. He was there at the time of the Biennale. He helped in a gallery owned by a woman called Glorietta who would leave him looking after the gallery while she was away. He stayed for the carnival in February and that is when the powerful and the influential recognised him as a threat. Glorietta always gathered friends together during that time and reserved a small theatre. From what he told me they celebrated the lives of writers, musicians and artists. Raimund took the opportunity to talk about the writers of South America, many of whom spoke out against the regimes there. If the seed of dissent was sown when he left for Europe, the flower bloomed in that theatre in Venice. He was on a list. The dictators love lists and he was near the top.

If you want to know more Jack you will have to find the diaries. Raimund loved the journeying. At the end of a day if he hadn't found a hotel for the night, he built himself a shelter. He spent a lot of nights in the open. Usually he stayed with people he met on the way. He met with locals, ate their food, drank the wine. He slept in meadows, walked over passes down to surging rivers, through woods and olive groves, never in a hurry, he wanted to observe his surroundings. He always talked of the immensity of the insect life, something that he had a deep interest in since a small boy on the pampas.

44

I found an address for Jurgen and Joseph and wrote a long letter. They replied within days of receiving it. Raimund had died in his house in Seville. Joseph had found him, on his lap was a photograph album open to six pictures of his family in Argentina years ago. The Rhapsody was playing quietly in the background. A picture of a surfer was on the table in front of him. "I think it was you Jack."

I walked to the veranda, my eyes full of tears. Looking out on the beach, in the distance there was a figure watching the surfers. I knew who it was.

He was buried in Colombia and one day I have promised myself I will visit his grave with Jessica. Apparently as they lowered him down, the noise from the jungle creatures was heard in the villages over a vast area. His influence is being felt in the world as I close.

And what of Jack? He and Jessica stayed on at the shack. I knew about their love for the place. He fished less and less and became more involved in the preservation of the sea which had been his life and had given him a living. I am sure you want to know who is writing this, well it's Joe, Jack's friend on the beach and on the boats. I visited the shack one early spring day. Jack and Jessica weren't there and their car wasn't out the back. I climbed the stairs to the veranda, peered through the windows, then saw a note pinned to the door addressed to me. "Joe, we've gone to the desert for a couple of weeks. There is something I am intrigued about out there, and I want to see if I can find it. I will contact you when we get home. Jack and Jessica."

I knew nothing of this and so would have to wait until they returned to find out. The two weeks passed, and then another two weeks, and another. I was worried for them. I did remember a caught conversation when Roberto had visited many years ago. " – yes, and I think I saw them one evening when returning to our camp, only a glimpse, but I knew they were there."

Never thinking much of the conversation and completely forgetting about it until reading the note left for me by Jack, it triggered memory. I awaited their return, and finally they did. They had been gone two months. I had seen lights on at the shack one evening. I went the next morning to see them and was greeted warmly by a wild looking Jack and Jessica. Two months in the bush had given them a well lived appearance.

I wanted to know what they had done and seen, and I had to wait until my third visit when they drew me into their wanderings over those months. When Roberto visited he spoke of a deep ravine far out in the desert where he had camped with an Aboriginal friend. They had remained at this campsite looking for a small bird, its predecessors having been slaughtered by the settlers. The little bird had, in the opinion of the settlers, ruined crops and spread disease. It must be killed and that is what happened, it was of no use. Jack and Jessica found the ravine and made a camp beside a stream that flowed from its walls. They had left their vehicle at the end of the track and walked a kilometre, humping their belongings to a rough shelter they had constructed.

That rough shelter became bigger and took on the appearance of a permanent dwelling. They spent longer in the desert and although I didn't know Roberto well, it sounded as if they had retreated as he had. Jack was irritated by my description 'retreated' and I understood why. He was looking for difference. He had spent his life by the sea and now was fascinated by the interior and the information he had gathered about the bird. This is what pulled him to the desert. The little bird represented survival. A survival that said 'I am still here, I will not be put down, chased, this is where I live and will continue to live.'

They travelled between the shack and the beach and

the ravine. The children were now adults; they visited, and absorbed the surroundings. Jack explored all corners of the ravine, scouring the walls, climbing to the top, walking the ridges, he found no trace of the bird. He spoke with the tribal people who frequented the ravine and the desert. There was little they could tell him, except to say that they had been seen several years back at the southern end, amongst high crags. Jack and Jessica set off to try and find them.

They started early one morning, it was going to be a long day, and by midday they found themselves on a narrow path amidst soaring pinnacles, and there far above, wheeling and diving, were the birds long thought to have been massacred. They alighted on the rocky outcrops and then continued their sky dance. Jack and Jessica gazed for minutes watching the display. Jack thought back many years to what Raymond had said, something about the swifts screaming and swooping around the roof tops in European towns during the summer. This must have been the same type of spectacle.

They had equipped themselves for a night in the open, finding a level plateau amongst the rocks. Meagre rations sustained them, the bed rolls softened the rock. Night fell quickly, they could hear twittering high up in the roosts, then quiet. The moon moved from rock gap to rock gap and then sunk, the sky ablaze with stars. Their plateau overlooked a high ridge, a gentle wind hummed. Towards daybreak they were woken by the soft padding of feet. A tribal elder stood looking down on them as they lay on the rock. She gestured that they should follow her and after packing their bed rolls, Jack and Jessica inched along a narrow path to an overhang that looked down to a waterhole and a rushing stream, the birds were whirling around the water, dipping down to drink.

"Sweet water," she said. She then told them about the water and the ravine, but first she talked of Roberto who had come here and understood the water and rocks. Sweet water, they went down to the pool and drank. The water was like no other water they had tasted. She said it was because a vast part of the country was crammed with gold, and this is what gave the water its taste and this is what the birds loved.

Prospectors had found the gold and realised the importance of the birds, in that they revealed the ravine and its abundance to others. They shot and poisoned, but a few remained and the small colony grew in size.

They stayed with the elder and whilst resting on a high ridge, in the distance out on the flats a plume of dust was rising. A car was approaching which took many minutes to arrive. It stopped, the driver emerged and Jack recognised Roberto slowly picking his way through the boulders to their position. Song flooded up to them, Roberto's arms were rising and falling in time, as he approached them, a tenor voice bursting from him.

Jack told me, "It was a moment which we will remember, Jessica often talks about it. The sun was high in the sky, the undergrowth crackling, the birds massing on the warm currents of air and this voice flowing up the rocks. I looked at the elder, who had a wide smile and was clasping her hands with pleasure. I felt she had experienced this before, and she had as she told me later." Jack became a defender of the country, as Roberto had been for years. The miners tried to appropriate the land, companies fought in the courts for their right to mine, they failed. Thousands of people took part in mass protests on the land, they occupied the heights and the ravines.

I started to lose touch with Jack, he spent so much of his time out there, when he came back to check the shack, he and Jessica would visit me. There was contentment in his manner, I knew that he and Roberto had won so far. The birds returned and the sweet water remained.

I raise a glass to them, Jack a man I loved for all sorts of reasons, and Roberto, well what can you say about him? When he died, Jack discovered a book in his house on the highway, it was his life, printed and bound, his life up to the week before he died. Who did that for him? We never found out.

There is a café, the best coffee I have tasted, on the highway south, it is called *The Northern Dancer.*

I visited it a week ago; there is a portrait of Roberto above the counter. I looked at it and then at the owner of the café. She smiled broadly and put her index finger to her lips. I like it that way.

Acknowledgements

The quote:

'You will win because you have an abundance of force, but you will not convince. To convince you need to persuade, and to persuade you need something you lack, reason and right in the struggle.'

is attributed to Miguel de Unamuno, Spanish essayist, novelist and philosopher, 1864-1936.

The quote:

the best kind of political system is run by wise old women appointed for their knowledge of the world and their judgement, uninterested in hierarchy, seeking the greatest good for the greatest number.

is taken from the article 'If you were an elephant' by Charles Foster, published by the Guardian newspaper 2017, and used with permission.

The quote:

"and kind things done by men with ugly faces."

is taken from *An Epilogue* by John Masefield, and used with permission of The Society of Authors as the Literary Representative of the Estate of John Masefield.

Printed in Great Britain
by Amazon